One Kiss At A Time

Maisie Robinson

Contents

Chapter 1

"Wait for me to come home,"

He used to say that every time he left for work. Every time his lips would hum those words as he leaned forward to kiss her. She did, always did and still did wait for him even though he no longer asked her to do so.

With white lavender perfume rubbed into her tresses, tired eyes of honey suckles would wait. Metilda whirled away in the kitchen, the hem of her light, cotton nightgown flourishing behind her like ocean tides. Her skin was pale and her heart was tired and sad.

Little Louis of five watched his mother heating the kettle of chamomile tea. It was his father's favorite, little Louis knew that. His mother always made his father's favorites because his mother loved his father very much. Though, he knew his father didn't love his mummy. He didn't kiss her like James's dad would kiss James's mom. He was always angry and shouted at mummy for no reason and sometimes mummy would yell back too. It made Louis very scared.

"Louis, why don't you go to bed? I'll tuck you in a minute." Metilda eyes were busy on the boiling pot of milk.

"Wait for daddy I want," Louis smiled at his mother, tugging the hem of her skirt. "Wait together,"

"It's not wait for daddy I want it's I want to wait for daddy together," Metilda had a rule of not answering Louis until he spoke correctly. Half the time, she used this rule to avoid his inquisition like why dad didn't come for dinner? Why dad didn't come to his school? Why didn't dad do this or that? Why does his mom cry? It gave Metilda a headache.

"I want to wait for daddy together," He repeated.

"No, he's going to be late again," In reality, Metilda didn't even know if he was going to return let alone be late. "There is some work left at office," She didn't even know why she was explaining all this to her son. "You know how hard daddy works for us,"

"Please mummy, Louis eat dinner with daddy,"

"My baby," Moments like these broken her heart. "If you go to sleep, I'll make you-"

"No!" He thrashed his fists in the air. Metilda noted how similar to his father he looked when he was angry. Their wild grass green eyes glowed red while their cheeks were tinted into the brightest shade of peach. "Louis eat with daddy! Louis eat with daddy!"

She sighed. There was no way to end his fit. Once he had begun throwing a tantrum, Louis won't calm down until he's gotten what he desires.

"Louis, you're a good boy. Good boys listen to mummy,"

"Louis bad boy! Louis bad boy! Louis eat with daddy! Mummy lies! Daddy, mummy fight! Daddy don't love mummy no more!"

She lost all self-control. Before even realizing it, she had slapped her boy. A moment later, red finger-prints appeared on his cheek. Tears crept out of her eyes, not Louis who had shushed up now.

She sunk onto the cold tiles, a blubbering mess of tears and sobs.

"Mummy, don't cry. Mummy, Louis be good boy now. Mummy, Louis go to sleep. Don't cry, mummy. Louis don't eat with daddy. Louis don't wait for daddy. I go to sleep. I don't make mummy cry like daddy. I love my mummy,"

Eyes drowned in tears, a heart burdened with sorrow, lungs breaking every moment, she hugged the small boy. Metilda knew in that moment she had make her son see that his daddy did love mummy. She would do whatever it takes.

Three in the morning, a fumble of keys resounded in the porch. A drunk, once handsome man stumbled into the one-story Houston house. Metilda rushed to her husband's aid. He laid a big, sloppy kiss on her mouth.

"May, June, July..." John slurred. "May, June, July... I can't never seem to remember their names."

There was a long strand of hair on his shoulder. It clearly didn't belong to him, Metilda noted, a bitter taste entering her mouth. Her young self would have been horror-struck. Her younger self wouldn't have let him in, she would have let him rot outside in the porch while she cried inside, right beside the door.

The smell of cheap perfume lingered from his coat as she placed it on the worn, maple dining table. John slumped onto the chair, a goofy smile on his lips. "May, June, July.... And Metilda,"

The strings in her chest tightened when he said her name. Right then, she knew she couldn't leave him even if she wanted to. Why was she being punished for loving him?

She poured him a cup of chamomile tea but he gripped her hand, stopping her in the process. "Why don't you leave me alone...?"

"You know why, John"

"I don't understand. We fight too much. You're making me ill, Metilda. Just leave me alone," He pulled her closer instead of letting go. Their breaths mixed as a snowstorm messed with the wild wind. With his index finger, he traced the outline of her lips.

"May, June, July. I can't never seem to remember their names but I remember Jannet and I love her,"

"I know you do," She whispered, calmly. As calm as a winter storm could be.

"She won't ever be mine until you take Louis's custody. She don't want the child,"

"Maybe that's why I don't take his custody." Metilda spoke freely. She knew he wasn't going to remember anything in the morning.

"Oh you evil woman, you pain in my-"He cursed. The words bounced off her stone hard shield. Whatever he said, it didn't make a difference on her anymore.

He pushed her away. "I'll get rid of you. I swear I will. Then I'll be free to be with my sweet Jannet and I won't ever come home,"

Metilda stroked his hair. It was as dark as the countryside's night sky. "You'll come back home, dear. Trust me. Love doesn't fall apart so easy,"

Chapter 2

After completing the article for Watcher's magazine, Metilda arrived at her son's school. By profession, Metilda was a journalist. She had a masters in journalism but couldn't fully pursue the career as raising her son took most her time. So occasionally, she would work as a freelancer and write reports for various publishing agencies.

The town's clock struck one fifteen in the afternoon. In her mother's red dress, Metilda talked to her sister on the phone while she waited her son's class to be dismissed. The school's front lawn was crowded with parents. Some chatted with each other, others were busy on their phones, and few stared off in a distance.

"Talirha," Metilda whispered, quietly. "I've decided. I'm signing the divorce papers,"

Her sister's frantic voice came from the other side. "Give it some time. I'm sure it'll be fine,"

Time was the one thing that Metilda wished hadn't slipped.

"It's not going to be 'fine',"

"But you guys were perfect. John, I can't believe he would give up on you easily. You two were the ideals for our marriage. Jai and I, we gained strength whenever we saw you. How did it fall so quickly?"

Metilda closed her eyes, her mind taking her to a place buried in the past.

John leaned forward, slowly. "You're my only one," His face was inches away from hers and then he whispered. "I love you and will keep loving you until death does up apart,"

Metilda felt her mind whirl further ahead as another scene played in front of her eyes.

The city lights sparkled, his entire face glowed with happiness. "This is our home. Can't you see it? The sofa will be here, the TV there and the kitchen, wow! Amazing, isn't' it? You've always loved to cook. This will perfect for us," He stopped walking and turned around, placing a hand on Metilda's belly. "And for our little one,"

Then another scene.

"Look what I bought you for Christmas," John slipped a diamond necklace around Metilda's neck.

Metilda frowned. "John, you shouldn't have. We need to be saving money. The bills-"

"Oh can we forget the bills for one day-"

"It doesn't work like that. We need to plan our expenses,

John tossed the necklace on the floor. "I sold my watch to buy you that necklace. Okay? Stop fretting out,"

Then another. Metilda wanted it to stop but it wouldn't.

"Why don't we go out somewhere this weekend? I mean we barely do these days," John smiled, hopefully one day after returning from work. "Let's go to the brookla-"

"With the baby and then my journalism assignments, I don't think I have the time," Metilda sighed as she heated up the baby's bottle.

"I'll take care of the baby while you finish-"

"No, John. I'll manage. The last time you gave Louis the wrong medicine and we had to rush to the hosip-"

"Never mind. Forget I even asked,"

"How did we fall apart so quickly?" Metilda mused. "It wasn't in one day, Talihra. Eventually small arguments turned into huge as the distances between us kept widening,"

Talirha stayed silent. "Are you sure there's nothing you can do to save your marriage?"

"He loves her."

"Who?"

"You know who I'm talking about,"

"Jannet" Her sister couldn't conceal the hatred in her voice.

"I don't blame her," Metilda sighed. "She only comforted John when I wasn't there for him," A gentle breeze tossed strands of golden hair off her shoulders. Nearby, another parent watched her talk, catching onto few words from her conversation. It was Daniel's father, a widowed man. His wife had died from leukemia four years ago, leaving their small but bright girl in his hands.

"You're too kind. You wouldn't see her fault even if it hit you in the face,"

"Talihra," Metilda's voice was as gentle as humming bird hovering over a nectar filled flower. Daniel's father's eyes were in a daze as he watched Metilda's red dress flutter with the wind. How beautiful, how pure she was.

"What?" Snapped Talihra. She never understood her older sister's strict morality.

"I've told you this before. I hate how always the other woman is labelled as the home wreaker. Jannet didn't wreak my home. If the walls had been strong enough, John would have resisted her."

"Have you heard of the saying too much goodness isn't good?"

Metilda laughed. Daniel's father swore that he had an angel sing. Maybe this was a sign, he thought, maybe it was sign that he should approach her. Listening to his instinct, he walked over to where she stood and tapped her shoulder.

Coincidentally, Metilda ended the phone call at the same time as her sister, who was a nurse practitioner, had some patients to see. This just confirmed Daniel's father's suspicion. Their meeting was meant to be.

"Hi there," He smiled, politely. "Louis mother, aren't you?"

Metilda returned his smile. "Yes, I am. Sorry but I didn't recognize you,"

"Reed Smith, Daniel's father. My daughter often talks about Louis."

"Well that's nice," She smiled, silently wishing that she knew something about Daniel. Louis barely talked about any of his friends. He would occasionally talk about James and his parents who were deeply in love and needed no excuse to kiss each other.

"I heard you're filing a divorce against your husband,"

Metilda rose an eyebrow. "And that is your business how?"

Reed held up his hands. "I'm lawyer that's why I was asking," Both Metilda and Reed knew that was a clear lie.

She narrowed her eyes at him. "Were you eavesdropping on my conversation?"

"Well, a poor man can't help what he hears,"

"Kindly, refrain from 'hearing' the next time around,"

"So there will be a next time. Maybe in coffee shop, south down Brookelen lane. What do you say, beautiful?"

Her eyes widened, as she paled significantly. "Are you-?" She shook her head. "Just because I'm getting divorced doesn't give you the right to pursue me."

The lawyer tucked his hands into the pockets of his trousers. "Why not? Your husband won't care. He isn't blind, is he? Only a fool would leave someone as beautiful as yourself,"

Metilda's skin became hot and prickly. She had always been bad at things such as flirting and persistent men. In her college days, she was often stereotyped for a bookworm. No-doubt, she was a shy, booklover.

It always amazed her how John had broken her walls. He was the life of the college, loud and friendly. Majoring in criminology at the time, he was something different. There was a natural charisma he had, the kind that would make anyone turn around and look at him twice.

They had English together. He would always contribute to the class discussion even though half the time it was utter nonsense while Metilda even though she had numerous, brilliant ideas sprouting inside her head, stayed silent. Metilda remembers how he had asked for her help on an essay and how thankful he had been afterwards. John wasn't the kind who would forget a favor. He helped her back and tried boasting her courage to speak up in class.

They started out as acquaintances and slowly, without even realizing it they had become so much more.

"So what do you say? It's a date." Reed broke the trance Metilda had been in.

She was about to respond and burn some sense into Reed when she felt an arm twist around her waist. The bright, afternoon sun sharpened the contours of John's face as he glared at the lawyer.

"Stay away from her. Am I clear? Or Do I have to make myself?"

Reed Smith, the lawyer and Daniel's father glared back. "Who are you, sir? And more importantly, why should I listen to you?"

John, in his tight, grey waistcoat and long overcoat, patted his trousers. Even as a detective for the local police, John rarely ever threatened the victims. Today, he made an exception. The silver revolver case fastened to his belt sparkled in the sun. Reed gulped and backed away.

As soon as Reed was a safe distance away, John removed his arm from Metilda's waist. To her great disappointed, Metilda longed for his arm to stay there. Even for a few seconds, she had felt safe and sound.

"You didn't have to threaten him. I could have handled him by myself," Metilda stood stiffly by his side while John's sharp eyes scanned the school's playground.

"Yah, right." John scoffed, running a hand through his night dark hair. "Handle it. You've been hopeless with men,"

She knew it was true but it did hurt her pride. "Maybe I've gotten better. How do you know? We rarely talk."

John eyes lingered to meet her gaze. He lifted his hand and ran it across her cheek. Metilda was tempted to close her eyes. "Your skin is warm, warmer than usual. It usually becomes hotter when you're tensed or nervous. If you had gotten better then you wouldn't be tensed. Would you?"

He retracted his hand, almost as though she were poison.

"It's best if I learn." She looked in another direction.

"You won't be there tomorrow and I won't have a reason to keep them away."

"We haven't gotten divorced yet,"

"Not yet," She whispered. "You're so determined. I won't be surprised if that day comes soon."

He didn't reply and she wished she could read his mind.

"What are you doing here?" She asked him. He never came to pick Louis.

"An investigation is going on the school's principal. We're trying to keep it undercover until anything is proven. I should get going." John briefly looked at Reed then back at Metilda. "Call me if there's trouble."

"Can you come home early? I need to discuss something important."

"I'm going out for dinner with Jannet," John bluntly replied. Metilda tried very, very hard to not let his words hurt her.

"It's pretty important." She shrugged. "The choice is yours,"

"Fine," Without another word, he left her. Once again alone. Little did he know, fate was going to make him scream with regret for every second he spent without her. Humans are strange. If they only knew how to value the present.

Louis of five years hugged his mother as soon as school was dismissed. Few feet away from them was

James and his parents who were laughing like a happy, little family should.

"How was school?" Metilda smiled at her little boy.

"Fantastico," He swung their linked arms back and forth and back and forth then he stopped and stared at James's family. "Where's daddy?"

Metilda's eyes automatically followed her son's stare. "He's here,"

Louis ear's perked. "Daddy,"

"Well, he's inside. He would visit us if he could,"

Instantly, Louis's face sobered into sad expression. "It okay, mommy. Louis understand it. Daddy work, daddy busy all time. It okay."

Metilda could almost grasp the longing in her son's eyes as she watched him stare at James and his happy family. James's father quickly kissed James's mother while James beamed at his parents.

In that moment, Metilda knew what she had to do. She stroked her son's head as the plan began to form in her mind.

CHAPTER 3

Seven in the evening, John stood at the door step of their cozy, one story house. Spring was about to arrive. John noted that he had few weeds to pluck from the front yard. The sunflower buds were almost ready to bloom. Metilda loved sunflowers, John reminisced, he had sown an entire patch in-front of their house just for her.

He rapped his knuckled against the door. The sound echoed through the small house.

Metilda opened the door a minute later, her skin flushed red, her brown hair in wispy curls.

"You came?" The statement sounded more like a question from her lips as she side stepped to let him in.

He hung his coat on the rack and shrugged his shoulders. "You told me to come. So here I am,"

She shook her head slightly. "I didn't expect you to come,"

He turned around and stared at her. "Why is it such a surprise?"

Metilda purposely didn't answer his question. "What about your dinner with Jannet?"

"I canceled it."

"Why?"

John rose an eyebrow, incredulous. "You said you had to talk about something important,"

"Oh of-course," She felt stupid for asking him that. She had been in such a daze from his arrival, she had no clue what she was saying. "I'm ready to take Louis's custody."

Relief filled John's face. "That's great news. God, Jannet will be so relieved."

Swallowing the bitter taste in her mouth, she smiled. "But-"

The smile dropped instantly as he interjected. "There's always a but. What do you want? Money, this house."

Tears swelled in her eyes. Is this what he thought of her? She blinked a couple times. The shield of strength and cold ice was back in place. "No, I don't want any of it. Keep your house. I'm capable of buying another for my son and I."

"What else do you want, Metilda?" He asked her, puzzled.

She took a deep breath in. "I want you to kiss me in-front of our son for twelve days,"

John didn't ask her why. He was afraid she would change her mind if he did. After three months of pleading, she had finally given in. Twelve kisses if that was all it took to get rid of her then so it be.

He stepped forward, eyes of green forest and honey met half-way. Before Metilda had chance to stop him, he lowered his face and captured her soft lips. It had been a while since he had last kissed her, a while too long. Metilda felt her heart race, faster and faster as he gently cupped her cheek.

No, no, no she chanted inside her head not now, not when their son was sleeping upstairs.

She did what she had to and pushed him away. "Were you listening to what I was saying? In-front of our son-"

John brushed off her comment with a bored expression. "The faster we get this done the better. One down. Eleven to go."

He started walking towards his room, leaving Metilda angry and frazzled. How she wished that kiss hadn't dazed her?

Before entering his room, he turned around one last time. "If you think in these twelve days, I'm going to fall in love with you again then you're heavily mistaken."

Was John always this cruel? Metilda thought because she no longer recognized her husband.

CHAPTER 4

John was sitting at his desk when Jannet walked into the cabin. In her tight police uniform and a revolver around her waist, she looked like an angel ready to kill.

"Any updates on the elementary school case?" She asked, tossing a red file on the table.

John sighed and shook his head.

"Darn," She pressed her palms on the table. "We need to get some leads on that principal before things get out of control."

"I won't let that happen." He placed his hand on top hers and smiled. "So officer, how was your day?"

"Tiring. Just came back from the East Bay patrol. Yours?"

"I have good news for you," He grinned.

She rose an eyebrow. "Really now?"

"Metilda agreed to take the custody,"

Relief flooded Jannet's striking features. She ran over to the other side of the table and hugged John. He wrapped his arms around Jannet's waist. They pulled away a minute later. A strange look glazed John's eyes. For a second too short, he felt unsure if they were doing the right thing. Why was he feeling this way?

Jannet clasped her hands together. "That's great news. You know John, I'm not mother material. I know nothing other crime and theses guns. It's relief that your son won't have to suffer with a horrible step mother,"

"You're not horrible. Plus it's for the best if Louis stays with Metilda. I don't think they belong in our world."

Jannet gave John's shoulder a gentle squeeze. "You've got me. I've got you. That's all that matter for now. Let's not talk about them,"

"Yah," John stared at the computer screen blinking before him. "Let's not talk about them."

"John," Jannet spoke after a moment. Deep down she knew no matter how hard she tried, John's heart would never belong to her. "You're over Metilda, right?"

John met her scared stare. "Of-course, I am." He stood up, straightening his long, grey coat. Jannet was about to lean down and kiss him but he quickly uttered the first thing that came to his mind. "I've got to go. I'll do some more investigation on the case."

"Okay, be careful."

John didn't know why he hadn't told Jannet about the twelve kiss deal. John didn't know why he was lying to Jannet. Once he was outside the police department building, he took a deep breath to calm his agitated nerves. "What the heck is wrong with me?"

"I'm hurting, baby, I'm broken down. I need your loving, loving" Metilda sang along the radio, her hips swaying with the beat as she whisked the cold butter. She was so engrossed in making the pancake batter and jamming out to Maroon 5 that she didn't notice the opening and closing of the front door.

"Sugar. Yes, please. Won't you come and put it down on me? I'm right here, 'cause I need. Little love and little sympathy"

Noticing the commotion coming from the kitchen, John walked into the dining area. To his great surprise, he found his wife, dancing and twirling around. Dressed in a floral chiffon top and capris, her curves flowed under the nearly transparent top.

Was it the heat? Or was this room getting hotter? John loosened his tie. God, when did his wife become so damn hot. Had she started working out or something?

He removed his coat. A droplet of sweat trickled past his brow. This was going to be a-lot harder. Especially, when his wife was so irresistible.

The soles of his shoes clicked on the tiled floors. Metilda turned around suddenly, her breaths caught in throat. Her honey spilling eyes widened. The hungry look in John's eyes. Damn.

He slipped his hand around her waist. Metilda's arms tightened around the bowl, holding it between them. "What are you doing?" She spoke sharply.

John blinked, once, twice. "What?" His breath smelled like tea and peppermint.

"What are you doing?" She repeated, removing herself from his grasp.

"Um...there was...some batter on your face." John brushed a finger along her jaw.

"I've been cooking for ten years."

John backed away, holding up his hands. "I was just doing what the deal required me to do,"

"Not now, later. In-front of our son. Don't make me repeat that."

He nodded. He couldn't wait to kiss those ruby lips. When John realized what he had just thought, he shook his head violently, his pulse rising.

What the hell did he just think?

"I'll come home early," John quickly went to living room and grabbed his coat from the rack.

"Wait, what?" Metilda came after him. He wished she hadn't. His body was reacting in ways he thought he had forgotten. Oh, those curves, those eyes, those lips. He couldn't stop staring at them.

"I got to go."

"But you just got here. We have to go pick Louis from school."

John wanted to get out of here as fast as he could. "I'll be there for dinner."

He slammed the door in her face, leaving Metilda stunned and frazzled. "Did I do something wrong?"

CHAPTER 5

As promised, John arrived in time for dinner. He parked his1998 Mercedes Benz behind Metilda's red Camry. Louis was playing with the neighbor's six year old girl, Bo. The kids were drawing chalk daisies on the sidewalk.

Bo shook head, her ink black hair falling out of the bow. "No, no. Loewis, flowers are not green,"

Louis glared at her. "Flowers be green."

"Mrs. Mole said flowers are not green," Bo crossed her arms over her chest.

Louis stomped his feet. "Louis want green flowers."

"I'm not playing. Goodbye." Bo flipped her hair and started walking away. Her sandals flopping on the side-walk.

"No," Louis ran after her, the chalk fell from his hand. "Wait, don't go, Bo."

John laughed to himself as watched his son chase after the neighbor's daughter. The woman is always right he thought he better learn that lesson.

He opened the door of the house. To find Metilda sitting by the dining table, a thick pad of paper by her elbow and a pen stuck behind her ear as she typed out an article on her laptop. Even in her messy, dismantled state, she looked gorgeous.

She met his gaze, startled. She seemed to be surprised a-lot these days. Was he really that bad at keeping promises? "Sorry. I haven't started on dinner yet. My back had been killing me. I'll start on it now."

"No, chill." John placed his coat on the rack. His wild green eyes took hers in.

She breathed out a shaky breath as he walked to her side. Gently, he pushed her back in the chair. He smelled of worn leather and Valentio, it was Metilda's favorite scent. She wondered when he had started wearing it again. "You okay now? Do you need to go to the doctor?"

"Yah, I'm okay." Metilda felt her shoulder brush against his waist. "I already went."

"What did the doc say?"

She shrugged her shoulders. "Nothing much. He prescribed me some pain meds."

"You rest. I'll cook dinner." John rolled up the sleeves of his grey shirt. He took a knife from the dish stand and started chopping onions. "Would you like onion soup? That's the only vegan dish I know how to cook." He flashed her a dazzling smile.

Metilda had an urge to fan herself as her cheeks got flushed red. He remembered.

"Are you still a vegan?" His grin dimmed slightly.

She nodded, not finding the voice to speak. Quickly, she averted eyes to the laptop screen. Her vision had become blurry. Why John, after all this time, why now?

In Metilda's checkered apron, John served a very hyper Louis and solemn Metilda dinner. He stood by Louis's chair and poured him a ladleful of onion soup.

"Yummy food, daddy." Louis bounced in his chair, nearly spilling the glass of orange juice.

"It's really nice, John." Metilda gave him a half-hearted smile. "Thank you."

"Oh, come on." He smiled broadly. "Stop being so formal."

He came to Metilda and served her some bread. "Eat up, love. You've gotten so thin."

And then, he quickly planted a soft kiss on her lips. It was enough to make her toes curl. "Ten more to go," She whispered to him.

Ice glazed John's eyes.

Louis grinned at his mother and then at his father. "Daddy, you come for dinner every day?"

Metilda's heart fell. "No, Louis. It is Daddy, will you come for dinner every day?" She corrected him, trying to buy John some time to answer.

Louis turned his hopeful gaze at John. Big, green eyes watched him. "Daddy, will you come for dinner every day?"

John ruffled his son's hair. "If that's what you want,"

"Yes!" Louis shot up in his chair and jumped merrily around the dining table. "Yes! Yes!"

Metilda gave John a disgusted look. "Don't make promises you can't keep."

"I intend to keep this one." He picked up Louis's dishes. "Whether you like it or not,"

While John tucked Louis to bed, Metilda scrubbed the dishes. Angrily, muttering to herself, she poured a handful of dish soap onto the sponge. "Who does he think he is?" She squeezed the froth onto the greasy plate. Bubbles danced around her red tinted face. "That bastar-"

She stopped mid-way as she felt a hand snake around on her wrist. "I'll do the dishes." John wrapped his arm around her and stole the sponge from her hand. Metilda felt her pulse rise up. He was so close, his front side pressed against her back. She turned around.

Wrong move.

Her face was inches from his chest. The front side of his shirt was stained with dish soap from her hands. John lowered his neck to her hair. Metilda's eyes widened.

He breathed in her scent. "Did you always smell this good?"

She paled significantly. Oh, dear lord. What was happening?

"Tell me," John's wet hands trailed along her waist.

The sponge slipped out of John's hands. He pushed Metilda against him. Their bodies were flush, her chest pressed against his.

"You're driving me insane, Mel." He planted soft kisses on her bare shoulder. She drew in a sharp piece of air.

The lines between lust and love beginning to blur.

And then he passionately kissed her, Metilda's back was pressed against the sink. Her heart gave a painful thump inside her chest. A blissful soared inside her as his fingers slid beneath her chiffon top.

"Not here," She gasped.

His strong arms swept her off her feet. He carried her to his room, refusing to let their lips part.

Chapter 6

John placed Metilda on the bed. He pushed her against the headboard. Their hands roaming in places which hadn't been in explored in a while. He moaned softly in her hair and as if coming to her senses, Metilda jerked away from him.

She wrapped the blanket around her body. "Must be nice to have two women at your service?"

John looked at her incredulously, feeling as though she had slapped him. He ran a hand across his face, the haze in his mind deepening. He couldn't get himself to think straight.

"What the hell are you talking about?" He got up from the bed. The streetlights from the window danced off his bare chest.

"Forget it," She turned around but he caught her by the wrist and pushed her against the wall.

"I can't do that." He whispered.

When she didn't reply, he added the next part. "No, I haven't slept with Jannet. If that is what you're asking me."

"You know, John, I know all your weakness. You want me now because I'm letting you go."

"I'm curious. Why all of the sudden you're ready to take Louis's custody?"

Metilda smirked. It chilled John to the core. There was a dead light in her eyes, a lack of life. "You don't love me anymore, do you?"

"No." He replied in a firm voice. I never stopped loving you he thought.

"You won't forgive me, will you?"

He averted his eyes. "You should go,"

She spared him one look before walking away the little dignity she had left. John collapsed onto the bed. His head in his hands, he groaned. "You're a bloody idiot, John."

John printed out the background verification papers of the elementary school's principal, Warren Thompson. Tired green eyes scanned the page. He hadn't slept a wink in last forty hours. Since he couldn't sleep, he thought he might as well come to work. That's the best part of working for the police, they don't put any time restrictions on you. As Sargent Sheffield said "It's about the quality, son not the quantity."

John weighted the thirty page stack in his hands. The ADI service department had really outdone themselves this time.

He scanned the narrow print. Nothing important came into view. Then his gaze stopped at a certain block of information.

[Prev⊠o⊠s occ⊠p⊠т⊠o⊠s] T⊠⊠v⊠lle Pr⊠so⊠ c⊠se м⊠⊠⊠⊠⊠er: ye⊠r 1989 то 2000

Developмe⊠т⊠l T⊠⊠v⊠lle Pr⊠so⊠ Psy-cн⊠⊠тr⊠c Dep⊠rтмe⊠т: ye⊠r 2005*-2010 (*e⊠rolled ⊠⊠ Mo⊠⊠т F⊠ll colle⊠e ғroм 2000-2005)

PнD ⊠⊠ ed⊠c⊠т⊠o⊠ овт⊠⊠⊠ed: ye⊠r 2011-2013

Pr⊠⊠c⊠ple oғ Кeтp⊠l Eleмe⊠т⊠ry Scнool: ye⊠r 2014-prese⊠т (*⊠o тr⊠ce⊠вle loc⊠т⊠o⊠ вeтwee⊠ ye⊠r 2013-2014)

"No traceable location, huh?" John leaned back in the leather chair. "Not much of proof but what the heck was he doing then?"

This was probably one of the most confusing cases John had ever dealt with in his career of six years. The entire case was built on one small detail. On 23rd February, three in the morning, an extremist group's call was received on Warren Thompson's cellphone. The content of the call: unknown. After that the police has been keeping track of his IP address. Not much suspicious activity there, the old man mostly visited the school's website.

John picked up his phone, hoping to text Jannet Good morning. It was a sort of habit he had developed over the past year.

March 5, 2015 the phone's screened blinked. John twisted the ring around his finger.

"Metilda" He breathed out as his mind took him down memory lane. "Today was the day Jannet took your place."

John paced infront of the emergency room. His aunt was in a critical state. She had a cardiac arrest in her sleep last night. John didn't know what to do. Other than Louis and Metilda, Aunt Rein was the only family he had left. She had raised him as her own son when his parents had died in an accident.

Trembling, John reached for his phone and dialed Metilda's number. He waited and waited for her to pick up but she didn't. After his the twentieth try, John gave up.

The police officer who had brought Aunt Rein to the hospital walked over to him. John recognized her from the police department. Jannet was her name. They had met a few times and were causal acquaintances.

John hated a stranger to see him in a blubbering mess. Jannet placed a hand on his shoulder. She didn't say anything, she didn't need to. Support was what John needed at the moment.

Two hours later when the doctors announced his aunt dead, Jannet was the one who held John in her arms while he cried. She was the one who stayed by his side at his aunt's funeral. She was the one who picked up John's broken pieces as he fell apart.

"I wasn't there for him." Metilda spoke with Tara at their favorite tea shop. The black ink haired woman frowned.

"You tried your best. It wasn't your fault that you had gone for an assignment to the Caribbean's. You guys needed the money then."

"That's not the worst part. I purposely left my phone at home. I just wanted a break from him. I just wanted to clear my head and rethink our relation."

Tara didn't seem surprised by the piece of information, or atleast she pretended not to be. The only time her sister does something selfish is the time when her husband needed her the most.

"There is still hope," Tara whispered.

"No, there isn't."

Tara stared at her sister. "Metilda, why do I feel like you don't even want to try fixing your relation with him?"

Metilda gazed at the golden ring around her finger. "Maybe I'm tired, Tara. Maybe I don't have a reason to fight anymore,"

CHAPTER 7

Metilda sat in school hallway, reading the districts magazine lying around. She was waiting for Louis and his class to return from their fieldtrip to the aquarium. Few other parents and grandparents were waiting for their kids as well.

Sadly, Reed Smith, Daniel's father wasn't among them. Metilda had been wanting to apologize to him for John's rude behavior.

She took a deep breathe in, the school smelled of mold and rotten meat. It took Metilda all her willpower to not gag at the smell. She looked around the compact hallway, the upholstered chairs and medals and trophies siting in the dusty cases. They really didn't clean this place, did they?

"Hello?" Metilda's gaze met dull grey eyes. The school principal was hovering over her petite figure.

She shifted awkwardly in seat before standing up. "Good evening, Mr. Thompson."

"How are you, Metilda?" He held out his hand for her to shake. She took his sweaty hand and gave it a firm shake. Warren Thompson was a chubby, old man with pepper grey and black hair. He had a friendly demeanor, the kind that made anyone feel right at home.

"I'm fine. The weather's been quite chill for spring, hasn't it?"

Warren nodded in agreement. "It has. So how's Louis? The last time you came to my office you were quite worried about him," It was true. She was fiercely protective of him. So when Louis came home, crying that his teacher had yelled at him, all hell broke loose.

"The homeroom teacher's actions were justified, I suppose. I mean Louis can be a really naughty sometimes. He shouldn't have dumped paint on that small girl."

The sides of his eyes crinkled as he laughed. "What is a child that isn't mischievous? Your husband must have a hard time with him. He works for the police, doesn't he?"

Metilda wondered how he knew about her husband. Then shook off her doubt, thinking that he was the principal. After all they have access to that sort of information.

"Yah, he's a detective."

Something flashed in his eyes, a tad bit of unease which he quickly concealed with a jaggery sweet smile. "Well, I know who to call if we have trouble."

John was having trouble. Nothing was adding up. The principal was a suspicious character. Why was he visiting the school website over a fifty times a day? No man in the world took his job so seriously.

Clicking on the Ketpal Elementary School website, he scrolled through the page. It seemed like a pretty dull website. Maybe on the surface, maybe there was something hiding beneath. John rung up the IT department.

Samuel also known as lazy ass, answered. "Ello?"

John contemplated if he should ask him for help or not. Considering how slow he was, it was better if John did the work himself. "Sam, bring over the Tech servers and encryptors."

"Planning to hack some account, sir?"

"Yup."

"Well, it's better if you come to the IT department and use our computers. They have a better processors than the ones at your office,"

Like John had said, Samuel was a lazy ass.

After an hour going through various interference and codes, John finally hacked into the principal's school e-mail account. His suspicion had been true. The principal had been using the school website.

He e-mailed his fellow partners the time of the meeting on the school website and then encoded a chatting system to the school website. After each chat session, the chat system was removed. There was no better way to hold extremist group meeting than that. No-one was going to doubt a school's website.

John opened the latest mail received on the Warren's account.

M☒☒☒☒H ☒☒$_2$☒$_1$☒

M☒ss☒☒☒ R☒☒☒☒s☒ B☒☒☒☒s.

☒☒☒ ☒F Adl☒t☒m

"Adlitem?" John thought out loud. "What is that?"

"Spelt backwards. Oldest trick in the book." Samuel who was munching away on a mayo sandwich, muttered through his open mouth.

"A-d-l-i-t-e-m. Spells Metilda." Samuel wiped the salad from his mouth. "Metilda, who's that?"

John's eyes widened. "That's my wife."

He shot up in his chair. "Sam, call the police. Red alert at the Elementary school."

She was going to be the bait for Mission Release. John had to get there before anything happened to her. If anyone lay a single finger on her, John was going to make sure they never see daylight again.

Speeding at 120 miles an hour, John arrived at the Elementary school. All was quite. He brought out his gun and walked into the school. In center of the hall, stood a crazed Warren with a revolver pointed straight at Metilda.

Metilda was on her knees. Not a trace of fear in her eyes.

John was the one who had fear captured in his eyes.

CHAPTER 8

For John, it was one those moments where he was having a hard time breathing. Metilda in her pale yellow dress sat on the brown carpet while a small huddle of terrified parents stood behind her. The kids were probably still in the bus. John knew the police must have reached out to them by now.

Warren dug the cold metal deeper into Metilda's neck. "If I were you, I'd put that gun down."

John smirked. Yes, he had the guts to do so when his wife was in mortal danger. "Sadly, you aren't me."

Metilda's light gaze watched John with a certain dullness. It was as if she didn't care if he saved her or not. Somehow that pained John. Did she not have a reason to live?

"Warren," John focused his eyes on the old man. "What exactly are your demands?"

"We'll talk about demands when you put down your weapons." Unwillingly, John placed the gun on the ground.

"Now shall we?"

Warren smirked, the old man that seemed friendly moments ago now had a sinister aura surrounding him. "You shouldn't be asking me. Mr. John, being one the highest paid detective of this area, you should have the answer by now."

"Mission release. What is that about?" John eyes darted in different directions. Warren's left arm was snaked around Metilda's shoulders and his right hand was on the gun. Any sudden move John made would take seconds for Warren to respond to. The parents standing behind could sneak up on Warren but that would be too dangerous.

Someone had to make the first move.

"Just as it sounds," Warren grinned. "Release our prisoners,"

John focused his stare on Warren. "And who exactly are your prisoners?

"Tom Henderson, Jake Mengite, Roy Mczhoky." These men were imprisoned for attempt to murder the senator of Westinhall. John felt like an idiot for not putting these piece together earlier. The school principal, Warren Thompson, was part of the Eleigt, an anti-government group. His experience at the prison center and then he after his PhD, he went missing- all had been pointing at this. In December of 2013, the attack on the Senator had taken place, the same time he had gone missing.

John stared at him blankly. No-way was the government was going to release them. Not until it came to the very last.

"That won't happen,"

A glint of anger sparked in Warren's eyes. "Then this will happen." He pressed his fingers into Metilda's shoulders. She nearly yelped out of pain but bit her bottom lips till it began bleeding. A single drop of blood dripped down her lips.

John balled his hands into his fist, veins in appearing on the surface of his skin. Desperation was all he felt right now. He wanted to whisk Metilda away from here, to a place where they used to be together. Safe and sound. Away from the eyes of the judgmental world, away from the harsh realities of their broken lives.

After their English II class, John walked along Metilda. The college halls were glittering with Christmas decorations. They stood in the student lounge where a gigantic Christmas tree had been placed. The student government club members were decorating the tree in blues and silvers.

John belonged to a family of atheist. He was always amazed by the beauty of religion, never having the chance to explore it himself.

Vincent Nguyen,who was leaning against the highest step of the ladder, dropped a silver garland from above.

The garlands tore into tiny, silver sparks from the sharp pine needles. They filled Metilda's hair who began laughing uncontrollably.

John glared at Vincent. He had feeling that he had done it on purpose. After all he had a massive crush on Metilda. "Watch it, will you?" John shouted at him.

Metilda shook her head, still laughing. "It's quite alright, John." Then she smiled at Vincent. "Do you guys need any help?"

Vincent gave John a smug look. "Of-course, help is always appreciated."

Metilda began helping Sarah string popcorn garlands beneath the Christmas tree. John plopped down beside her.

"Can I help too?"

Metilda bit down on her bottom lip. John noticed she did that whenever she wanted to laugh but couldn't or whenever she wanted to cry but didn't.

"Here." She handed him a thread with a needle stuck at its one end.

John drew his eyebrows together. "I don't know how."

Sarah scoffed. "You must be joking."

"I'm not." John replied, sourly. Metilda eyes caught the momentary loneliness in his eyes. Her cold hands wrapped themselves around his sweaty ones. "I'll show you how,"

Afternoon turned to evening, the sky went from blue to orange as piece by piece Metilda and John built a garland for their very first Christmas together.

"Call your police department head." Warren spoke. "Tell them about our demands."

John did as told to. He put the cell phone next to his ear but Warren barked to put it on loud speaker.

John held the phone in front of him. The monotone ring buzzing through the air.

"That was unprofessional of you, John," Was the first thing, Chief Bentel said. "To approach the culprit without orders,"

"Sir, with all due respect, I am very sorry. We have a situation-"

Warren groaned loudly. "Will you cut the chase and get to the point."

"Sir, you need to release prisoners Tom Henderson, Jake Mengite, and Roy Mczhoky."

"The ones who attacked Senator Roderick. Impossible"

Warren's eyes widened and for a second his hands slackened on Metilda's shoulders. It was finally donning on him. The government wouldn't release criminals that were a threat to the national security for a handful of civilians.

Alert, Metilda used this opportunity. She jammed her elbow into Warren's groin. He jumped in surprise and fired the gun. The bullet shot the trophies resting in the dusty cabinets and the glass shattered.

Chief Bentel's panicked voice filled the room. "John, Is all under control?"

Metilda shot up on her feet and tried knocking down Warren. Warren may be old but he sure had a-lot of strength. His right hand fixed in the air by Metilda's strong grip , he tried to fight off her voracious attack with his left hand.

John as if coming out his stunned state and picked up his gun. He couldn't fire with Metilda in such close proximity with Warren. He tackled Warren from his back side, causing the gun to slip out of Warren's fingers and land on the floor. Metilda quickly seized the gun and tossed it far from Warren's reach.

Few of the parents rushed to help John keep Warren pinned to the floor.

Breathlessly,John handcuffed Warren's wrists who was squirming relentlessly. "I hope you enjoy your stay Mr. Thompson."

Warren scowled, his gums were bleeding profusely from Metilda's power-packed punches. "I'll get you. I swear I will."

In walked the police officers, late as usual. The officers took control of Warren. There was a chaos as parents were being rushed outside by the police. Only two people stood still in the chaos. John and Metilda, eyes locked in the others, both were breathing heavily. Metilda was still ghastly pale from the aftermath of the incident.

Officer Blake was talking to John and Officer Melissa was interrogating Metilda. They were separated by few feet. Just few small steps and all distance would vanish.

Slow steps were made by John as he approached Metilda. His lungs, his heart were dying to hold her in his arms, to know she was safe.

When the first step was completed, Jannet barged into the school hall. Long, flowing locks of black were trailing behind her, eyes of blue oceans glistened with tears.

"John! John!" She chanted, her voice broke in-between. She fell into John's arms. Metilda's eyes still held John's. She wasn't going to let him affect her.

Her eyes were glassy, her face was flushed red from effort to keep the emotions buried within.

Challengingly, she smiled at him. Appearing the happiest and relieved she could enact to be.

Even though, she wished she could be the one held by his strong arms and breathe in his strong scent.

But then Jannet pulled away and kissed him hard on his lips. John nearly fell backwards by the impact. He kissed her back nevertheless. It took him a second, to forget about his wife who was standing few feet away.

Jannet was always there for him and that's all that mattered.

Not his wife, who he was about to lose moments ago.

Once Louis went outside to play with the neighbor's daughter, Bo, Metilda rushed to the bathroom. She had been holding herself together for too long, smiling and laughing with her son, appearing calm with the officers.

She poured out some painkillers and chugged them down her parched throat.

"I don't care. I don't care. I don't care." She whispered over and over again. "I won't cry. I won't cry. I won't cry."

Slowly, she sunk onto the cold tiled floors and then screamed into her hands.

Cheeks stained red, eyes that no longer held happiness, stared blankly at the wooden cabinets.

...If only there had been painkillers for the heart...

Chapter 9

The sun was bright, the clouds had settled on the ground as dew. John removed his shoes outside the door. His aunt hated when he brought in mud with his shoes. He removed his long, mustard trench coat and set it on the sofa.

Few minutes after walking aimlessly though the house, he found his aunt. She was sitting in the library. John breathed in the scent of old books, rotting papers, and dust. In the sunlight, specks of dust danced. His aunt's library was old. It had been passed down from one generation to the next. The furniture was at-least a couple decades old. The upholstered chairs were now falling apart as cotton seeped through the fabric.

Aunt Rein, a portly woman, sat on the maroon rugs. A screwdriver and grease bottle in her hands. She was taking out bolts of an old radio. The antennae was bend at an awkward angles and the back lid was open.

John plopped down beside his aunt and rested his head on her shoulder.

Instantly Aunt Rein turned her head. "Oh dear boy, when did you come back?"

"Just now." He sighed.

"Long day?"

He simply laughed. "You have no idea." Then in a serious expression, he whispered. "I almost lost Metilda today."

She smiled sadly. "But you didn't"

"I didn't. I was scared though. Really scared. For a moment, my heart had stopped beating. You know, aunt that feeling of losing someone you lo-... I can't describe it."

"Ah, the doings of love. Brings pain if the other is in it."

John didn't reply. He simply stared at his aunt, lost in thought as her deft fingers tightened the bolts of the radio. In a gentle, soft voice, his aunt began singing the song she often sang him to sleep with.

"Blow the wind southerly, southerly, southerly,

Blow the wind south o'er the bonny blue sea;

Blow the wind southerly, southerly, southerly,

Blow bonny breeze my lover to me."

John closed his eyes. The weariness of the day escaping him.

"They told me last night there were ships in the offing,

And I hurried down to the deep rolling sea;

But my eye could not see it,

Wherever might be it,

The bark that is bearing my lover to me."

"This radio keeps breaking," His aunt sighed, setting the radio in a standing position

"Why don't you throw it out? I could always get you a new one." John spoke through half open eyelids.

"What can be fixed shouldn't be thrown." There was a strange peace in his aunt's eyes. "It was your uncle's. He would often tune into the news about the wars. Then when he left me to serve the nation's Navy, I would sit in his chair, listening to the war's news. It was my only solace in the days when he was so far away."

"What if it can't be fixed?"

"Maybe," She stroked his hair. "You don't want it to be fixed."

"Why would I want that?"

"It would be easier to get a new radio, wouldn't it?"

She smiled at him. And then meaning of her words finally settled in.

John woke up. Sprawled on a grubby sofa, it took him moments to adjust to the light. He was in Jannet's apartment. After the incident, Jannet had brought him to her house. He hadn't protested, not wanting to hurt her.

He shifted on the sofa, coming to a sitting position. Jannet sat on the loveseat opposite to the one he sat in. She was intently watching a football match.

"You're up?" She asked him, when she noticed his gaze upon her. "Should I get you something? Water? Juice?"

John was pretty hungry but he wasn't going to ask Jannet to cook. Let's say she was lacking in the cooking department.

"No, I'm fine."

Jannet sat back down. "Well, how are you feeling?" Metilda probably wouldn't ask him that question, she would wrap her arms around him and rest her head on his chest. One glance and she knew what he was feeling.

"I'm okay."

Jannet gave him a close lipped smile. Being in the police, she rather not talk about unpleasant encounters. After all, that was what surrounded her average day. "Elise couldn't believe it," Jannet changed the topic. "that I am going to the New Year's party with you,"

"What is there not to believe?"

Jannet walked over John, a sly smile on her lips. "You really don't know, do you?"

John raised an eyebrow as she placed a hand on her hips.

"You're one of the most coveted man in our entire police department," She pushed his shoulder gently. "Sir, women think you're H-O-T,"

John wondered if Metilda still found him attractive. The way her eyes glazed over him, bored, uninterested- he didn't think so.

"You flatter me too much. There's nothing like that,"

"And that's the best part of this. You're so oblivious to all the attention,"

John glanced at the clock. 9:13 p.m. it read. Had it been five hours already?

"Jannet, I'd love to talk but I've got to go."

She stood up as he did. "Why? Your wife won't be missing you,"

"But my son will,"

John walked into a silent house. He roamed through the house, room to room searching for Metilda. He found painkillers scattered on the bathroom floors, dishes piled up in the sink, food left on the dining table. Clearly, Metilda wasn't expecting him to come home.

He checked in Louis's room and finally found her. Cuddled next to their five year old son, Metilda slept soundly. She snored softly, light brown wisp of hair falling off her face.

John walked to the bed. She looked so innocent. So did his son.

He leaned down and planted a kiss on his son's forehead. Before he could stop himself, he kissed Metilda's cheek. Her cheeks were wet from tears. She had cried herself to sleep.

"I'm sorry, Mel." With his thumb, he wiped the last trailing tear from her lashes. "I should have never let you go."

CHAPTER 10

Metilda woke up to an absolutely clean house. Every room was vacuumed properly. The pills that had been scattered on the bathroom floor were neatly arranged in a pile on the counter. Metilda walked into the bathroom and threw the pills into the trash. They weren't effective anymore. Her back still ached last night. She was going to ask the doctor for a higher dose.

Pulling the light pink robes closer to her chest, she made her way to the kitchen. To her very surprise, the kitchen was sparkling, the dining table was absolutely cleared of the plates and food from last night.

To her shock, John was making pancakes. He whisked the batter in a blue bowl and ladled a spoonful of batter onto a steaming pan.

Yesterday, when Metilda had seen Jannet take John's hand and take him to her car, she didn't think he would come home. Yet here he was, handsome, freshly shaved face, hair combed to one side. In a forest green t-shirt and khaki shorts, he looked stunning.

Though Metilda never loved John for his physical appearance, she still adored his attractiveness.

"John," Metilda briefly glanced at the wall-clock. It was nearing to eight-thirty in the morning. He usually left by eight. "Aren't you going to work?"

When John's eyes met Metilda's, he was breath-less. There was a dull ache in his chest. She is alright, she is alright. But every time John closed his eyes, he would see Warren pointing a gun in Metilda's direction.

He tightened his grip on the mixing bowl. He want to hug her so badly. "No, I'm taking the day off."

"Why?"

"I thought I might." He hesitated for a second. "Spend the day with Louis and you. We could go to the beach or something?"

"This isn't part of the deal."

John averted his eyes. "I know why you have that deal. I know you want Louis to think we're a happy family and there's no better way to prove it than a small outing."

"Louis has school today,"

"No, school was cancelled for the investigation. They want to make sure that the school is absolutely safe."

Metilda knew school was cancelled. She just wanted to get away from John. Only God knows, how much more her heart can take.

"Aren't you going to help in the investigation?" John wanted to laugh for a moment. It felt as though Metilda was interrogating him.

"I think I've done enough already."

She stared at him for a moment then turned her back to walk away.

But before she could set a foot outside the kitchen, John had wrapped his strong arms around her. Metilda dug her hands into his shoulder, her head buried in his shoulder. They stayed like this for a long time. Both their eyes were welled with unshed tears.

"Are you okay, Metilda?" He whispered, unwillingly he moved back.

She nodded.

"I still care for you,"

"Of-course, you've grown attached." Her eyes were stormy. "One can grow attached to a dog."

Horrified, John took a step towards Metilda. "You're not a dog,"

I sure feel like one Metilda thought. This time as she left him, John didn't stop her.

Ocean waves fell upon one another. The beach was fairly empty, considering the slight chill of spring and it was a Tuesday. The sand felt nice under her bare feet as Metilda, John, and little Louis of five walked along the shoreline.

"Daddy," Louis who stood between his parents, his hands linked with theirs. "I grow up, I have a big house here."

"No, Louis. It is when I grow up, I will have a big house here." Metilda automatically corrected him.

John ruffled his hair with his free hand. "And so you will."

Louis beamed at his parents. "Really?"

John leaned down to Louis's level. "If you work hard, you will have all that you dream."

"Louis will work hard," He spoke with determination.

"Good boy." John kissed his cheek then he rose and kissed Metilda's cheek. It was quick but it was enough to make Louis squeal with happiness.

"In my big house, I will live with mommy and daddy."

This time Louis spoke with perfect grammar and suddenly, Metilda felt as though she wasn't needed anymore. It was a strange motherly kind of fear but it was overpowered by the joy of her son and her husband finally bonding.

Chapter 11

After a long, patient walk at the beach, John had taken his family out for mashed potatoes and burgers at The Cullen's which was a forty-five minute drive from Galveston bay. The drive had been a joyous and cheery even. John and Louis played I spy while Metilda watched them with a content smile on her lips.

Then after lunch, Louis had fallen asleep and instead of having an awkward silence fill the car space, they had an actual conversation. Yes, John and Metilda talked like the old times. He was careful not to bring up anything that would call up unpleasant memories.

The radio played a beautiful Alan Powell song and all was perfect. The wind slurred through Metilda's hair and John's finger tapped the steering wheel to the beat of the song.

They talked, talked, and talked about rodeo, country music, and the strange names of Texas cities. It all blurred in Metilda's mind, half their words, half of John's flirtatious smiles.

"When I first saw you, I was like Damn, what I can do to get me one of those," John grinned.

"Are you kidding me?" Metilda laughed.

"You are quite attractive." He drawled the word. To his sweet satisfaction, Metilda's cheeks were rosy red. He had purposely said are instead of were.

"What were you thinking when we first met?" John steered the car towards I-75 exit. Home was so close.

Metilda bit the side of her lips.

Metilda was standing alone at the freshman's party. Most of the kids were busy staring at each other, some were actually bothering to strike up a conversation. John was one those few. A large cup of Dr. Pepper in his hand, he grinned at a bunch of senior gals.

Metilda made her way to the refreshment table. She came to this party out of boredom. 'Might as well stuff up on the food', she thought. At the same moment, John- a green eyed, black haired boy- spilled Dr. Pepper on her.

Metilda loved Dr. Pepper in her mouth, not on her clothes.

"Eh," The guy bent over on his knees to pick the cup. Metilda was enjoying the view until he came back up. "Really sorry about that, miss."

"It's alright."

"No, I'm really sorry. I wasn't watching where I was going. Is there anything I can do to make it up?"

Were all Texan guys this polite? Being a New York girl, Metilda wasn't used to this kind of chivalry.

"No, I'm fine."

"Please, let me make it up to you. I could buy you a new dress or something?"

"A spin in the washing machine and this dress will spotless. Plus its black, it won't stain."

"Take it off."

Metilda's eyes widened. "What?"

"Wait that came out wrong?" He looked mortified. "I mean I'll wash it when you take it off."

"Sir, you are an idiot and I will not take off my dress." With that she walked away.

To Metilda's great displeasure, she had English class with the same green eyed boy.

"So what were you thinking?" John sneaked a peak at her face.

. She brought the heels of her feet to the seat and wrapped her arms around the leather boots "That you were a perverted guy with a hella nice ass,"

That was the last thing John expected her to say. "I'm not perverted,"

"Really? John, do you really want to take me there?"

"Hey, hey. You make me sound like a crusty old man who has nothing better to do than watch girls walk by."

"Maybe that's what you are,"

"Please don't say that," John looked absolutely mortified. "People have enough reasons to hate me. Don't make that list longer,"

Metilda couldn't keep it in anymore. She burst into fits of laughter. "I swear.... (laughs)... you act like a... (laughs)... kid sometimes. Even Louis is better than you,"

Would it be a sin if I kissed her right now? John thought. The guilt of the situation caught up with him a minute later. What the hell was he doing?

When they reached home, the sun had settled behind the horizon. Metilda was fast asleep. She must be really tired because John didn't remember Metilda being one those people who liked to sleep when the sun was up.

Ah, the small things he remembered about her. He remembered every small detail. It's just that he didn't show it anymore.

John parked his Mercedes in the garage and the unlocked the doors.

First he carried Louis to his room. He quickly tucked Louis in and turned on the heart-shaped night light. Louis hated the darkness, just like Metilda did.

Then he went back to the garage, Metilda was snoring softly. He lifted her in his arms. She felt so light, almost like a fragile doll.

John carried her to his room. Even John doesn't know why he did that. She looked so breakable and he was scared to let her go.

As John laid her on the bed and removed her boots, he lost himself completely to the war inside his head.

He felt a hand on his shoulder. It was aunt Rein. She smiled, a strange sadness in her features.

"My child, forgive her. It wasn't her fault."

"I can't," he whispered.

"Just so you know, I've forgiven her,"

"You have a big heart,"

"For my sake, forgive her. I won't be able to rest in peace until you do,"

John looked back to see his aunt disappear.

That night John didn't sleep. All night long he watched Metilda sleep.

"What are you doing to me, Mel?" He spoke softly, in a hushed voice. "I thought we were done for good but then you come up with this deal. How am I suppose survive the next nine days when you've got me whipped by three kisses?"

He buried his head into the web of his hands. "I can't let you go Metilda but I can't stay with you either."

CHAPTER 12

Half-way through the night, when John had finally managed to fall asleep, a small, scared voice woke him up. There was something warm and soft on his chest. It was Metilda's head.

"Mommy?" Louis sniffled. He was standing at near the door's frame with a stuffed bunny in his right hand while the other gripped the door's edge. "Mommy, where are you?"

John got up carefully, not to wake up Metilda. It seemed like she had a peaceful sleep after ages, judging by the small smile on her lips.

"Daddy is here, Louis." John got up the bed. He picked up Louis in his arms who was shivering terribly. "What's the matter? Bad dream?"

Louis buried his head into the stuffed bunny. It had two black buttons for eyes. When Louis was two and half years old, he had chewed off the toy's eyes. Metilda tried getting rid of the bunny but he cried and cried for days without it. Defeated, she had stitched the buttons from John's old coat onto the bunny.

"Louis, what's wrong? Why are you crying?"

John asked as panic settled in. Louis wasn't one of those kids that cried easily. It took a-lot to make him cry.

"Are you pain? Is it hurting somewhere?"

Wide eyes of green looked at him. "It hurts a-lot, daddy"

John carried Louis to the kitchen and turned on the lights. He placed Louis on the kitchen counters who was now hugging the bunny tightly to his chest. As far as John remembered, Metilda kept children's Tylenol in the glass cabinet.

"Where does it hurt, Louis?"

John felt his head for a fever but it was normal.

Louis pointed to his chest. "In here, daddy. I feel sad."

John stopped rummaging through the cabinets and turned to his son. "Why do you feel sad?" He wasn't good at this sort of things. Metilda, as stereo-typical this may be, was always the better one with kids.

"You and mommy were fighting in angry voices. Then daddy, a big evil monster came and took my mommy away. Louis fought with the monsters and told them not to take his mommy away but they still did. I called for you, daddy. I told you to save mommy but daddy, you gone away."

"Nothing like that will happen, Louis. I won't let any evil monster take your mommy away."

"Angel's promise?" John wondered when Louis had caught onto Metilda's habit. Metilda believed in angels, demons, and those sort of mythical beings. She believed that no matter what, even in the direst of circumstances- God sends an angel. May it be in a form of a human or a simple signal, idea, or thought.

An angel's promise, according to what Metilda had told him, is a promise whose safety relies on angels. Human beings aren't capable of keeping promises, an angel's promise is when something or the other will happen to guide you back to your promise.

John had made one such promise to Metilda. On the evening of their wedding, when they sat by the cackling fireplace.

"You're my only one, Mel." John whispered and kissed her forehead. "For forever and always"

"Forever and always." She held out her hand for him to take. "Angel's promise. So I'll know no-matter what happens, we'll always find a way back to each other."

"Why are you so adamant on those promises? Don't you believe me?"

"I do, John, I do but who has seen the future?"

He sighed and looked above. "Whatever angel is watching us right now, please help us keep this promise."

Metilda smiled. "That wasn't so bad, was it?"

John smiled back. "Actually, it is kinda comforting."

"I told you."

"I promise." John gripped Louis's hand. He wanted to know if Metilda still believed in these promises after all that had happened.

Louis let go of the bunny and hugged his father. John held him close. This divorce was going to break his child apart.

Was it really worth it?

The answer was a clear cut no.

Metilda woke up with Louis nestled in her stomach and a long arm draped around her. It was John's arm. What in the world was she doing in his room, on his bed?

She shifted slightly, the digital clock read the time to be a quarter past eleven. Blinking a couple times, she tried remembering what day it was today.

Wednesday- Louis school was off until Thursday but John, why is he still here? Doesn't he have to go to work? John isn't the type to take a day off. Why now? The last time he took a day off was two years ago when I had a fever.

A blush crept to Metilda cheeks as she remembered the day. Her insides felt warm and fuzzy.

It was really sweet of him. What a darling he used to be.

Another part of her mind argued. He still is a sweetheart. He made dinner the day before yesterday.

Metilda hesitated for a second before resting her fingers on John's forehead. Touching him, felt like fire. A fire was burning deep inside her pit. She looked at her hands to make sure they hadn't been burned black.

She brought her hand to his face and traced his jaw.

At the same moment, John's eyes flew open. "Metilda?" He croaked. Her stomach flipped over. He had that gorgeous morning voice.

Instantly, she pulled away. "John, aren't you late for work?" She hid her face in the waves of brown velvet hair.

"Oh," He slowly positioned himself to a sitting position. Louis was sleeping soundly between the two. "What time is it?"

"Eleven eighteen."

He breathed out a deep sigh. "I'll work from home. I don't think Chief will mind."

Metilda watched him for a moment. What are you up to, John?

Louis helped his father plant sunflower seedlings on the empty patch of soil near the porch. John's brow was thick with sweat. The sky was clear and the evening sun was hot and humid. Spring was in full blow.

Birds were chirping sweetly, the crickets creaked, and the honey bees buzzed through the air.

Metilda stepped out, wearing a flannel shirt and blue jean overalls. In the bright sunlight, she looked paler than usual. Her hands trembled as she carried two bottled filled with mustard colored liquid.

"I brought lemonade." She handed one bottle to Louis, whose hands were icky with mud and another bottle to John who had been shoveling the soil to create proper patches for the flowers.

"Thanks." John spoke as he set the shovel aside. "You alright?"

Metilda nodded her head. "Yah, just some allergies."

"You don't have pollen allergies."

"No, I developed mild sensitivity to them after Louis. The doctor says it's nothing to worry about."

"You take care. Okay?"

"I will," Metilda leaned against the wooden railing of the patio. "You guys need any help?"

Louis looked up, grinning as a Cheshire cat. "Mommy, look what I found?"

There was a fat, long earthworm wiggling in his fingers.

"Louis put it back. You're hurting the poor thing."

Leave it to Metilda, John internally smiled, to be concerned for a worm.

Louis tossed the worm back into the soil.

All was silent for a sometime while John and Louis finished their drinks. The wind blew Metilda's hair haphazardly. Her skin glowed slightly, her eyes shined with a joy that had long been missing.

And John swore under his breath that there had never been a more beautiful sight.

Louis walked up to his mommy and handed the empty bottle. "Thank you, mommy. It was yummy."

Metilda leaned down and kissed his cheek. "You're most welcome,"

John handed the bottle to Metilda. He was about to kiss her cheek. There was a mischievous glint in her eyes and she turned head. Their lips met half-way.

She instantly pulled away.

"What did you do that for?" John asked her, breathless by just a brush of her lips against his.

She smiled, shyly. "I wanted to."

He stared into her eyes, which were so deep and entrancing. The distance between them seemed to vanishing. The eyes of honey were pulling him in, into a never-ending whirlwind of passion and love.

He was about kiss her again when a loud slam of a car's door interrupted them. Jannet got out of her 2001 Honda Civic, fiery expression on her face.

Metilda looked in between John and Jannet, panic settling itself in her chest.

"Louis," She quickly grabbed her son's arm. "Let's go in and wash your hands. They've gotten so dirty."

"Mommy but Louis didn't finish putting baby plant in the hole,"

"It's okay. Daddy will take care of it."

She picked Louis in her arms and rushed inside.

Metilda turned on the tap in the kitchen and placed Louis hand's under the running water. From the kitchen window, she could see John and Jannet arguing. She speed walked to the window and closed the blinds, shutting out the evening sun.

Before she had closed the blinds, she had seen John get into Jannet's car. And all she wanted to do was run and tell him.

"Don't go, please."

CHAPTER 13

When ice blue eyes met wild green ones, John knew he was in trouble. Big trouble. He hadn't told Jannet a single detail.

He didn't feel like talking to her anymore.

Jannet. Jannet. May, June, July, it doesn't matter anymore. He didn't care.

She was in her police uniform. Slim, curves in the perfect places, light brown skin, black hair. She was in her attack position. She had a habit of doing that whenever she was angry, frustrated. John wouldn't be surprised if she was thinking of hundred ways to kill him.

Light honey eyes caught John's attention. Metilda rushed Louis inside, her short brown locks bouncing on her shoulders.

Jannet stopped in-front of John.

"What were you doing?"

"It's not what it looks like."

She grinded her jaw. "Not what it looks like. You were about to kiss her."

"There's a park down south street, let's talk there."

"Why not here? And why did your wife walk away like I'm some disease."

"Please, Jannet. No drama, please."

"Oh, okay fine." She snapped her fingers. "Plus we both know who the drama queen is."

She was talking about Metilda. John didn't contradict her, knowing that she was right.

[six months ago]

John was feeling absolutely blissful. He was getting promoted to a higher official position. It meant he no longer would have to rely on chief's order to run an investigation. He could request for a search warrant using his own name and he would get an entire department of detectives and policemen under his control.

Another reason for his happiness was Metilda. Yes, he never thought he would use happiness and Metilda in the same sentence but she had accepted Jannet's truth without a word. She just stared at him when he told her that he wanted to divorce her because he had fallen in love with a police officer.

John released a deep, content sigh. The police department was holding a small reception for him. He was on cloud nine that day. A group of officers, chief Bentel were congratulating John. It was the proudest moment of John's life.

Jannet had her arm wrapped around John. She was beaming at him as the officer's congratulated him.

In walked, Metilda. The numbness from yesterday had faded away. There was a range of expressions on her face, from sadness at John's betrayal, from anger at another woman holding her husband's arm.

She wore the sultriest black dress in her closet and the darkest blood red pumps. Her thighs were exposed and so was her midriff. John felt boggled at her attire. His Metilda never dressed sexy, never.

The entire party of men was staring at Metilda. She walked as a fierce lioness, her eyebrows draw in a tight line. John could feel Jannet's arm loosen around his arm.

"You?" Metilda pointed at Jannet. "Keep your hands off my husband,"

John's eyes widened. Hell, no. Metilda was here to humiliate him. She was finally going to retaliate. "Mel, come on. Don't create a scene."

"Don't call me Mel. How dare you! How dare you cheat on me? Just because I didn't pay attention to you for a week, you found yourself another women. You!" She jabbed her finger in his chest. "You! Narcissistic, arrogant, egoistic, attention hungry jerk."

"Metilda. Not today!"

"John," Jannet gripped his hand. John closed his eyes. No-one can save him from Metilda's wrath now. "Do you want me to talk to her?"

"Who the hell are you? I'm talking to my husband." Metilda barked.

"Your soon to be ex-husband," Jannet quietly added.

"Oh, where were you when he was struggling? Now that he has the cash, you chase him down? You filthy gold digger!"

"Metilda!" John screamed. "You've crossed your line. We're done. Why can't you understand that I'm tired of you? I want you out of my lif-"

Metilda's palm collided with his face. "John Hamington! I am not a piece of clothing that you can throw out of your life."

John was too stunned and embarrassed to say a thing.

"Congratulations, Mr. Detective."

As she walked away, one of the junior police officers stopped her. "Can I have your number?"

She glared at him. "Go to hell."

John made sure to note his name so he could fire him later.

"A twelve kiss deal? Why the heck did you agree to it?" Jannet wrapped her hand around his arm. Few parents were watching over their children from the benches. Jannet and John too sat on one such bench except they were staring off into a distance as the sun settled over the horizon, scattered with a few trimmed shrubs.

"She's clearly trying to win you back."

"I wouldn't be so sure." John wanted to place some distance between their bodies. Jannet's entire left leg was pressed against his right leg. Somehow it felt wrong.

"What do you mean?"

"Think about it, Jannet. It's been six months and now she's suddenly agreeing to take Louis's custody."

"You think she wants your son to think that you're one happy family. What's the point of that? I mean, your son will eventually find out the truth."

"Jannet, Louis is five years old. I don't think any five year old boy needs to know that his parents hate each other's guts."

Ice blue eyes gazed into John's eyes. Jannet wanted to kiss John right now but he wasn't holding her gaze. "Something has changed," She whispered. "John, I know you like mysteries. This exactly what she wanted. She became a mystery that you would want to solve."

"I'm just curious. Jannet. And you're overthinking this."

Jannet shook her head, laughing causally-even though her heart was sinking in her chest, how long will she able to keep his heart?

Then she brought her lips together. "I thought you were sick or something. John, I got so worried. You're so serious about work, I didn't think there would be a day when the great detective misses work because he overslept. What were you doing anyways?"

Watching Metilda sleep and trying hard not to fall in love with her innocent charm.

But of course he wasn't going to say that. "Watching a football match."

Chapter 14

[eleven years prior]

It was sunset time. The grass bellowed with the wind, rustling as it went. At the west harbor, the men were unloading their catch from the day. The sea whipped back and forth. The skies darkened. Sparkling like those beautiful, proud denizens in the sky, the sunlight danced off the water.

The best part of going to a college by the sea was the beauty. The oceans, the tolling of the bells, the flashing of the light house, the early morning shouts of fishers, it was all so entrancing. What was more enchanting than that?

Nothing.

Maybe there was one thing. Falling in love for the very first time.

"There is this girl," John whispered. He and Metilda sat on the deck by the sea. Their feet dipped in the water. "And my friend loves her like hell. She gorgeous, smart but well, my friend is quite good looking too but he's scared to ruin their friendship. You know love messes everything up. I don't know what to tell him. He's screwed. He can't love her, he can't be just friends with her,"

"He should just tell her how he feels. Kiss and tell. That would be so sweet," Metilda clasped her hands together. She was such a hopeless romantic. "Friends turned lovers, the perfect dream."

"So he should just kiss her?"

Metilda nodded. Her excitement resembled a small child's.

"Kiss the life out of her."

"Are you sure?"

"Absolutely!"

John got on his knees and kissed Metilda. Her lips were cold, soft, and sweet of the strawberry jam she had eaten.

Metilda's eyes widened. One minute John was sitting next to her, the next he was holding her arms behind her back and kissing her like she was the only piece of air left.

A fire burned so bright behind Metilda's fingertips. In the shocked state, she knocked John off her. He lost his balance and fell into the chilly blue sea.

Unfortunately, John didn't know how to swim. He gurgled the saline ocean water, his arms collided with the water. Drops of ocean surrounded Metilda. She jumped into the ocean and her arm under John's shoulders. Having lived by the sea all her life, Metilda was an excellent swimmer.

She dragged John and herself to the sandy shore.

John's lips quivered. His skin had turned a light blue. "Th-that was a cold rejection."

"I can warm it up if you'd like." There was a playful smirk in Metilda's eyes as she kissed the corners of John's lips and John felt air return to his lungs.

When Metilda kissed John at the dinner table the following day, he felt air return to his lungs. He felt alive at once. Every nerve, fiber, cell in his body was rejoicing in joy. It had been exactly twenty-eight hours since she had last kissed him. The festival inside his body quietened when he realized there were only seven kisses left.

Metilda left the dining room to tuck Louis into bed. And John was left alone to clean the table and dishes.

Metilda woke up half-way through the night. Louis was snoring softly and she had somehow fallen asleep in her son's room. She walked through the desolated house. There was music coming from the living room. She stopped near the entrance, her heart beating insanely fast.

It was their poem.

Everyone couple had one song or poem that belonged to them. Metilda and John had one too.

[ten years prior]

John had gone for the foreign exchange program and Metilda was missing him more than she missed her mama's home cooked veggie casseroles. It was a yearlong program in France where he would be staying with an unknown family.

Metilda was scared that John would fall in love with some devastatingly beautiful French woman and he would forget about her.

All her doubts and worries were put to rest by the arrival of a certain package. John had sent Metilda a chocolat-bayonne-daranatz.fr along with it had arrived a small cassette.

[present]

In the cassette, John had recited a poem for Metilda, a French poem.

"Mel, I yearn to hold you in my arms. France has many beautiful sights but nothing is as beautiful as your eyes. In the marketplaces, I heard a man sing this poem. My French isn't good and his English wasn't good either but somehow he managed to word all that I am feeling right now."

Metilda's heart swelled. Why was John listening to this old tape? All her thoughts dwindled away when she heard young John's voice once again.

"If sometimes when I am sailing on the large rivers, lakes I never sleep when distant memories track down me But the boat where I fled slides these deep waters And inexorably move away from what was this world.

The price of this passage is paid by these long absences That lead me to this country of refuge, hidden in the silence Where my feet will stop at the border Where I see the sky shining in my many prayers.

So, I will light the lantern before morning My happiness is there, between your hands."

Metilda walked into the living room. It was dark. The white curtains were parted by the window. Near the windowsill, sat John with the cassette player near his feet. The window was open and let in the cold drafts of air. His eyes were in a daze, wisps of black hair blowing along the wind.

"I was wondering," John didn't need to look to know Metilda was here. He could feel her presence as one could feel sunlight behind closed eyelids. "Where we went wrong?"

"Maybe it was for the best." Metilda wrapped her hands around her bare arms. "It's better this way,"

"I don't hate you. Metilda, I never did. Even after all you did, I can never hate you. My body just isn't programmed to hate you."

"I love you and I always will." He added after a moment of silence.

When John's eyes met Metilda's, the world had stopped spinning. Their wedding rings sparkled in the sparse amount of streetlight. For a moment, John thought he was standing at their wedding altar. The sound wine glasses clanging together filled his ears.

He wanted to hold her in his arms but couldn't.

She wanted to bury her head in his shoulder but didn't.

"Then why are you leaving me?" She asked him.

"I don't know anymore." He sighed.

She smiled at him sadly. If she could have one wish, she would wish for John to love her without feeling guilty about it.

"Sleep well," She bid him a silent adieu.

"I doubt I will." He muttered under his breath.

CHAPTER 15

On the day of the fifth kiss, all was happy in the Hamington household. Metilda was writing her report on the recent football match. John was helping Louis eat breakfast.

John watched from the dining room: Metilda's narrow back bent over the laptop, her eyes lost. She sat on sofa in front of the TV. A random new report playing on the TV. He knew for a fact that Metilda was having a hard time writing. He walked over to her while Louis placed the empty bowl of cereal in the sink.

Resting a hand on the sofa's back, John placed a feathery kiss on Metilda's cheek. "Everything alright?"

Metilda's heart fluttered, a bird that was about to take flight again. She knew she was falling in love with him again and she wasn't going to stop herself from falling.

"Yah." She lied sweetly.

He lifted her chin so she would meet his gaze. Metilda had an urge to raise an eyebrow. Seriously, why do you even care?

"Are you sure?"

"Yes. I am." She wanted to slap his hand away yet she wanted to also pull closer and steal all his breaths.

"If you say so. I'll be late today." John quickly added the next, seeing Metilda's thinly concealed disappointment. "Chief and I are going to South Harbor. There's been two murders in the area and they need our help." Why was he giving her explanations? He just wanted her to know he wouldn't be spending the day away from her with Jannet.

"Be safe." She touched his jaw then quickly pulled her hand pulled away realizing how close they were.

Louis was approaching the living room. His backpack tightly fastened over his shoulders. He was grinning at him parents.

"Daddy, let's go! Time for school."

John leaned down and kissed her cheek. Again. "Goodbye, I'll see you at night."

"Bye."

"Talihra"

The very beautiful women with star like hair smiled. Metilda was visiting Talihra's home. It felt less like a home but more like a temple with the different statues of gods and various incense sticks lighted in the hall.

The instant she stepped inside her house. All her emotions that she had bottle up from the past week burst through. She turned into a sobbing mess. Talihra held her sister and led her inside, to her room.

Talihra's room smelt of Sandalwood. They sat on the bed.

"Shh, it's okay. I got you. I got you." Talihra stroked Metilda's short, brown curls. "I got you."

After five minutes of crying, Metilda felt at peace. Talihra was a sort of person that could make anyone calm down.

"How's everything going?"

Metilda shook her head. "Fine. It's been going better than I thought it would."

Talihra smiled. "I told you. John's a great guy. The only time I wanted to rip his head off was when he brought Jannet to our reunion."

"Yah." Every year, Metilda and John came to Talihra and her husband's house to celebrate valentines. Few months ago, on Valentine's eve, John brought Jannet to Talihra's place. Talihra being her feisty self kicked John out the second she saw Jannet. "But you did tell him to get out of your house. It was amazing."

"Well, if my sister's husband brings his mistress to MY house, there are meant to be some casualties."

Metilda's smile broadened. She was glad Talihra was her sister.

They weren't related by blood. Their appearance made it clear. Talihra's tan skin and silvery hair juxtaposed with Metilda's honey colored eyes and brown hair. They used be friends in their college days that is until Talihra refused to acknowledge her as a friend but instead as a sister.

"I love you. Have I told you that before?"

"A million times. I'm going to do prayer now. You want to join?"

Even their religious beliefs were different but that never bothered them. Sometimes Talihra would go to the church with Metilda. Sometimes Metilda would pray to Talihra's gods.

"Yes, I want to ask them a few things."

Talihra's smile dimmed. She placed her hand Metilda's shoulder. "Everything happens for a reason. We have to keep our eyes on the light, not the darkness."

"It's hard to at times."

"I know it is,"

Talihra's god was dressed in light yellow silk. A garland of freshly plucked lilies hung around the golden neck of the god. He was beautiful in his black, bouncing hair and diamonds embedded into the embroidered dress.

The entire puja room smelled of sandalwood and roses. Metilda sat beside Talihra, her hands folded together.

The wind chimes sung a pleasant tune by the window.

"John says he loves me yet he wants to leave me. I know Jannet was the never the reason for the broken state of our marriage. We had fallen apart long time ago. It was like I was sleeping walking through our lives until one day I am jolted out of sleep by John's new relationship. By then it was too late."

Metilda took in a deep breath, kept praying harder than she had ever had.

"I was so occupied by the struggles. Every day was a struggle for me. I had Louis, then my career was on the rise. Things were hectic in those days. I don't know God when he drifted away. I don't know what to do anymore."

The wind rustled through the curtains. Metilda's eyes were dazed. She felt Talihra's hand on shoulder.

"Look what I found."

Metilda took the small note from Talihra's hand.

Forgiveness is the final form of love.

"Thank you," She whispered to the marvelous golden statue.

Louis was sleeping soundly in his room and Metilda was about to retire to her own room when she heard the front-door open. She wanted to go straight to bed, not in the mood to face John today, not when she felt so peaceful. But her instincts told her otherwise and she always followed them.

When Metilda walked into the living room, she found a bruised and bandaged John collapsed on the sofa. He was breathing heavily. His eyes had been bruised and both his arms were wrapped in a cast.

"Oh God," She ran to John. Her John, the first man to love for all that she was.

"I'm fine." He moaned. "I swear I am."

"You sure are." She forced John back into the sofa. "Stay. I'll make you some tea. It'll help you sleep and ease the pain."

"They already gave me morphine."

"Then be ready for that headache."

He sighed and collapsed back into the sofa. "Fine."

"How did it happen?" Metilda spoke through the kitchen. He could hear her pull out the kettle.

"It's not a very exciting tale if that's what you're expecting."

She turned on the tap and water rushed into the kettle. "I still want to hear it."

"I decided to outsmart the murders. They were hiding in a deserted outpost by the sea. Chief and I tried to force them out but they wouldn't come and kept on firing at us. I ducked under the car's hood to dodge the bullets. They eventually ran out of bullets. Somehow Chief and I managed to capture them and bring them to the police station."

"How did you fracture your arms?"

He grumbled something under his breath. "It's not a fracture, just a sprain."

"So how did it happen?"

John wished she wasn't so persistent. "At the police station, I slipped over a banana peel and fell down the stairs. Chief took me to the ER and drove me home."

Metilda started laughing. "The cunning detective is defeated by a mere banana peel. What a glamourous tale!"

"If you were the one in pain, it wouldn't be so funny."

She walked outside with a tray on which rested the kettle, a tea cup, and saucer.

"Your pain is my pain." Metilda whispered. She titled her head slightly, strands of hair fell over eyes. "It has always been. Even when Aunt Rein died. When you cried, I felt the pain."

John lifted himself off the sofa. His face mirroring the calm before a storm.

"Are you done?"

She grabbed the back of his shirt, preventing him from moving on. "Forgive me, John. Please."

"Let go, Metilda. This is the last talk I want to have with you."

When she didn't, John screamed. "I said let go!"

And she did. Metilda knew she had tried. She forgave John for all he had done wrong and now she knew there was nothing left to do but watch time take its turn.

Chapter 16

Another night, another sleepless John sat on the settee near the window. Forgive me. She had said. And he had said nothing.

He wanted to ask her: "For what? You never did anything wrong."

When John was young, he and Metilda had these idealistic views on marriage. They knew it was going be hard but they didn't know it was going to be this hard. Marriage for him was always about himself, his pleasure, his sorrows, his happiness but marriage is everything other than yourself. He realized it now. Marriage was about her happiness, her sorrows, and her pain. A successful marriage places the importance of the significant over oneself.

Thoughts like these made John's head hurt. If life could only be simpler.

He'll be more careful with Jannet. He'll make it about her, not himself.

But what about Metilda? Why couldn't he make it work with her?

Because all Metilda reminded him was the darkness in life, the arguments, unsaid words, mistakes, frustrations, and the screams.

He wanted to be in the light and Jannet was his light.

It was a lazy weekend and the day of the sixth kiss. Metilda ran the comb through her wet tresses. She stood by the door of the back porch. Wind softly rustling through her hair. The sunflowers shining in the morning sunlight. She usually woke Louis up by ten but it was ten-thirty right now and the poor child could use some rest. Schools these days tire the life out of children.

She wondered how John was getting ready, considering both his arms were sprained. She at-least expected a call for help from him. Maybe not, after all she had poured salt over some old wounds.

She laughed to herself. Of course, he wouldn't forgive her. He was one stubborn man. He could tell her that he still loved her yet he couldn't forgive her. And they said women are complicated, well then men are confusing asses.

John was getting ready to take a shower. It was ten o'clock and he never woke up this late. The lack of sleep in the previous nights must be catching up to him. There was one thing John hated and it was being asleep past the rise of the sun.

He stripped out of his office clothes, it seems like he had fallen asleep in them. His arms pained a bit as he lifted the shirt above his head. The joints of his elbows screamed with pain when he reached out of the toothbrush. He had to bite down on his lips to prevent himself from screaming.

Before stepping into the shower, he turned on the radio box. It was a strange habit he had, of listening to music while he showered. He has specifically gotten the radio box installed in bathroom for this reason.

"Welcome to 95.7 FM where we'll be playing the new release by MAGIC! Ladies and Gentlemen hold your breaths because this song will literally take your breath away."

He was about to turn on the tap when he remembered he couldn't get his bandages wet. He went back and shuffled through the cabinets, looking for something to cover his arms with. After searching for ten minutes, he found these arm length gloves Metilda used for waxing the bathroom tiles.

Pulling them on, he stepped back in. Steam engulfed him. The water was extremely hot, just the way he liked it.John felt the soreness from yesterday leaving his muscles. He turned his attention to the song playing.

"I am a sinner, as cold as the winter
She is the sun, she is the queen of love
I am a burden, always uncertain
She is a raft, only believes in us
And I know that she cries by the red in her eyes
She's been waiting for signs that never come
All she ever really wanted was...
One woman, one man
that's all that she asks
No other demands
One Woman, one man"

This song couldn't have had a worse timing.John groaned out loud.Seriously? Why was karma so bent on putting him down?

But then again, this song was true. For him, even though Metilda was no longer the sun. She still had been once upon a time, the sun, the empress of his heart. And yes, he had been the sinner. The colder one in this marriage.

John was forced to think back to the days when he had first announced his relationship with Jannet to Metilda. The red eyes of wine still haunted him at night. How could he be the same John? The young John could never bear a single tear in her eyes yet this John is the reason for the pain behind those eyes.

He couldn't do it anymore. The guilt, the tremendous guilt of putting down the person he had loved so much was suffocating him. John was about to step out, again, and turn off the radio. Some habits were better buried in the past. He didn't think he could listen to music anymore, not when every single song reminded him of Metilda.

Just then, something unfortunate (well, fortunate for those who hate John) occurred. The gloves John wore still had wax on them. The wax had melted from the hot water and dripped onto the floors. The shower door was half open when it happened. John set his foot on the trail of wax and kaboom, he slid back into the shower, his legs sprawled wide apart, the shower curtain on the floor, and his sprained arms pointing to the roof.

Wide-eyed and half in pain, John realized there was no way he could get up. The angle at which his body was stuck in the shower required both his arms to exert maximum amount of force to get up.

But being the stubborn man he is, he tried getting up. He was out of breath by the third attempt and his arms were throbbing as though on fire.

He had either two options: he could stay here all day long with the hot water pouring on his face or he could call for help.

Why was his ego so large? Chewing his bottom lip, John pushed his arms for the third attempt.

Metilda had just finished the report for Time's magazine and was about to head to Louis's room to wake him when she heard an irritated cry for help. What could it be?

"METILDA!"

She stopped at the door of John's room. "What is it?"

"In the bathroom," He replied, panting.

She cautiously walked to the bathroom, wondering what he could want. Hopefully, not what she thought because there was no-way she was joining him for a shower. He choose Jannet, not her.

Metilda didn't step inside the bathroom and stood by the door. "Is there anything I need to get you?"

He groaned loudly. Someone woke on the wrong side today. "Can you get in here?"

"Why?"

"You'll see."

"I'm not coming until you tell me."

Another groan. "I fell and now I can't get up."

She turned the knob. It was locked. "John, the door's locked. I'll go get the screwdriver."

"Just hurry up!"

After unscrewing five screws and two bolts, Metilda had finally managed to open the door. She was about to walk in when she remembered one small detail.

"You're wearing clothes, right?"

John scoffed. "Like you haven't seen me naked before."

She blushed red. Before Metilda could make some witty remark, John added. "I'm covered, just come in, I'm tired now."

"A little kindness wouldn't hurt," She sighed.

"Please, my beautiful wife, please help your husband who is in great distress right now."

She almost rolled her eyes at his sarcastic tone. God, they were arguing like two teenagers. She honestly wondered where maturity went, maybe down the drain.

"Coming in!" She announced. A large cloud of steam attacked Metilda. The shower was still running and John was squashed exactly under it. His legs were spread wide apart like he was doing splits and his shoulders were wedged between the door. The blue striped shower curtain had been cleverly placed over his manhood.

Thank god! he had some decency. She thought. He must swallowed a lot pride to ask for my help.

Metilda scratched the back of her ear. "How should we do this?"

"Can you atleast turn off the shower? My skin's all wrinkly."

"Oh, sorry." She quickly closed the tap and backed away from him.

"Now, can you help me? My legs hurt." John looked up at her. It is safe to say he's never felt so embarrassed in his life.

"Stop whining. You're annoying me."

"Well, it's all your fault. These gloves had wax on them. You should have cleaned them."

"First of all, did I tell you to wear my gloves? Second of all, do you have any common sense? No-one wears waxing gloves to the shower. You should have asked me and I could have tied a plastic bag around your arms but no, of-course, talking to me hurts your ego. Look now where your ego has got you."

"Mel," John softly whispered. Beautiful green eyes stole her breath as her pulse began rising. "I'm sorry."

"I'm sorry too,"

"I forgive you." For what? Metilda wanted to ask.

She found herself leaning to her knees and snaking her arms under his shoulders. "Let's get you on your feet, Okay?" Her fingers burned a trail through his shoulders. He had an urge to close his eyes.

Water drops clung to his black hair. She felt her heart race, freely and wild.

"On the count of three, I want you to try lifting yourself up," Her breath grazed his ear. He felt goosebumps rise on his skin. "One, two, and three..."

And they tried. John pushed his sore leg muscles and Metilda forced her tired arms to help him up. It was of no use.

"Let's try it again." She huffed and they did. This went on for ten minutes before both of them gave up. Red sores were beginning to sprout where Metilda's arms held John's shoulder.

"One second." She moved back and leaned against the tiled walls.

"Let's try something different." John chocked out.

She nodded and moved to stand behind John. Metilda realized that she would have to bring herself closer to him. Trying to calm her rapid breaths, she brought her elbows under his shoulder joints. His back was flush with her chest and she started lifting him again

John was beginning to slowly inch his legs together. He was almost on his knees, then a moment later, he was on knees, pushing himself upwards. Metilda's arms slowly left him and John stood on his feet.

Relief fled John like an avalanche. Without even realizing it, he was hugging Metilda- naked. The shower curtain now lay in a pile at his feet.

"Thank you. Thank you. I love you so much."

He kissed her hard on the lips, rendering her speechless. Honey light eyes stared at him, wild, surprised, and flustered.

This is when John realized he didn't have a single article of clothing on him. Metilda realized it too. Her cheeks were colored the brightest shade of red.

She looked away. "I-I'll go make breakfast."

John quickly put his hands over his private parts. "Ya-yah. I'll be there in a minute."

She ducked her head and ran out the bathroom.

Once she was outside, John began laughing uncontrollably. God, they've been married for seven years yet they're acting like a newly married couple. John remembered their first night. Oh, how awkward things had been?

"We have to do this, John." Metilda didn't dare to meet his eyes. "If we want kids,"

John clenched his stomach. Oh man, what an awkward, shy guy he used be in bed and Metilda was the total opposite, a tigress. She had to compliment him every time to boost his confidence.

It was a strange moment for a realization. As John laughed, he realized that they had more moments of happiness than sadness. It's just that, being human, John clung to the darkness rather than safeguard the light.

CHAPTER 17

At 2:30 in the afternoon, when John lightly pecked Metilda's heated cheeks as they watched the Sword in the Stone with Louis, the door bell rung. Metilda shot up and rushed to the door. She needed an excuse to get away from her John. She couldn't sit next to him without wanting to rip his clothes off.

To her not so much of a pleasant surprise, it was Reed Smith and his daughter, Daniel. Reed Smith was a tall and dark handsome lawyer and his daughter was a gorgeous five year old with long, curly black hair.

It had totally slipped out of Metilda's mind that she had invited Reed Smith for lunch over the weekend. Being the kind person she is, Metilda kind of felt guilty for John threatening him.

"Oh, come in Mr. Smith. I'm so glad that you could make it." She tried putting on her sweetest smiles. The lawyer seemed to be in a daze. Can she get any more beautiful? He thought.

"Louis, look! Your friend from school Daniel is here." Louis didn't budge from the sofa. His eyes were fixed on the TV screen. John, on the other hand, was bubbling with rage. What in the world was he doing here? Here he and his family were enjoying a movie like a happy family should but the lawyer had to come and smear the beautiful scenery.

He walked over to Metilda and stood behind her, his blood about to reach boiling point. "What are you doing here?"

"The lady invited us for lunch."

Metilda smiled at John. "I think Mr. Smith deserves an apology"

John glared at him. "Not on my watch."

"Well, then. You can take your moody self to the living room. Mr. Smith and I will have a nice lunch." Secretly Metilda was enjoying John's displeasure. He looked so very adorable when envious.

Metilda made her way to Louis and dragged him to the hall. "Louis, come on. Say hello to Daniel."

Louis, who like his father, looked displeased to have company, scrunched his nose upwards. "I don't play with Daniel. She makes me always be the servant."

Daniel giggled. "Silly, you're the pauper and I'm the princess."

Metilda ignored her urge to raise an eyebrow. "Be nice. She's our guest."

He made an ugly face. "No thank you. Louis stay with Daddy." Louis gripped his father's hand. John gave Metilda a smug grin that said see, even Louis agrees with me.

Metilda placed a hand on her hips, clearly not pleased with the scene the males in her life were making. "Fine, you two do whatever you please. Mr. Smith would you and your daughter like to have some cheesecake?"

"Louis want cheesecake too!" Louis pouted.

"Ask your daddy." Daniel stuck her tongue at him.

Metilda, a very ecstatic Mr. Smith, and his hyper daughter strolled to the dining room. John swore under his breath as he watched the lawyer purposely brush his hand against Metilda's thigh. If this continues for another second, there surely would be bloodshed.

"Daddy," Louis tugged John's hand. "Cheesecake?"

John sighed. His phone buzzed with a message.

[Are you alright, babe? I heard you fell from the stairs.] - Jannet

Another sigh left John's mouth. He didn't want Jannet's attention.

[Perfectly fine. Just a small sprain.] -John

[Oh! Do you want to come over to my place? I can take good care of you]

[I would but I think I'm going rest today. Thanks for the offer though.]

[Should I come over?]

Why was she being so insistent? John wondered. She must really missing him. At-least someone did. Metilda looked joyful as she served two chilled slices of raspberry cheesecake to the lawyer- the bloody liar.

John looked at down his phone screen. He typed: You know what I'm coming over. You stay where you are.

But just as John was about to press the send button, he felt slightly cold fingers wrap themselves around his hands. Metilda smiled at John and Louis.

"What did you think? I'm going to let my grumpy bears starve."

With her other hand, she gripped Louis's hand who looked just as thrilled as John was.

"I love you, mommy."

"I do too," John grinned. Once seated in the chair between the lawyer and Metilda, John quickly changed the message he was about to send to Jannet.

[Nah, don't bother. I'll be sleeping through the day anyways.]-John

Reed Smith left the Hampton household an hour later. He clearly had expected to spend some time with Metilda, not her husband. Metilda had left John to take care of their guest as she went to visit her sister. Reed Smith and John talked (yes, they had a civilized conversation-Reed was not a bad man other than the fact he was trying to steal John's wife) about the current affairs in politics while their kids played the princess and the pauper. This time Daniel played the pauper and Louis was the princess.

John stood outside on the patio's steps. Louis had a monkey grip on his neck and his small legs wrapped around John's waist.

"Wanna go for a ride, champ!"

"Yes! Yes! Yes!" Louis squealed.

John roamed around the neighborhood with Louis on his back. Bo's father, Chinh Phan, a portly Asian man with thick glasses, asked about John's sprained hands. John elaborately explained how it happened. The two men shared a hearty laugh.

"So?" Chinh sobered up slightly. Bo was riding her terminator's bicycle with Louis sitting on carrier. Both children made strange sounds as though they were on a rocket to mars. Other people on the sidewalk dodged the kids, small smiles on their face as they reminisced their own childhood.

"Is it true? You and Metilda."

Chinh's question jolted John out of the joy around him. The two men walked in silence for few minutes.

"It is." John finally answered. The sun was starting disappear behind the horizon, marring the blue sky into a teary red and black.

"Too bad. You had a wonderful family. I suppose things don't work out sometimes" John didn't like how Chinh talked about his family in the past tense. As though they already were doomed. It was true anyways. If not now, in the next few days they will fall apart.

"Can I ask you something?"

Chinh smiled, well naturedly. "Ask away."

"How do Asian marriages last so long?"

"Well, you're talking about my father's generation. I swear I haven't heard of anyone getting divorced in his time. Anyhow. When I got married, I was nervous as hell. A wreak. It was arranged marriage." Chinh laughed when he saw John's befuddled expression.

"It's not as bad as you think. I was introduced to Solida by my parents. We talked a couple times. I liked her. She was sweet, strong-headed, and a simple girl. Apparently, she liked me too. Lucky me."

"And then?"

"On my day wedding, I was planning to run away. I didn't think I was ready for this sort of commitment. Then my father came with words that literally changed my whole world: if you treat this relationship as a commitment then it will feel like you've been caged for the rest of your life.

"He looked into my eyes and said. My son, treat it like a journey, a beautiful journey you two have to make. If life were a boat, you two would be the sailors weaving carefully through the storms. She is a human, cherish her, love her, and always remember that she will make mistakes and so will you. You will have to learn to accept her for all she is.

"He smiled, an inside joke I didn't understand at the time. I know your generation has set an expiration date on marriage. Such a thing never crossed the mind of your mother and I. We couldn't even think of such possibility. It's such a bizarre thing for us. The day we got married, we both knew that we were in it for the rest of our lives. I can't imagine a day without your mother and I don't think she can either. I hope you and Solida find the same kind of love that we did."

John breathed a long sigh. His eyes misty. "Wow."

"He's an amazing man." Chinh wiped a tear from the corner of his eyes. "I miss him at times. You know being so far away from Vietnam. I haven't seen him in two years."

John placed a hand on his shoulders. "I can understand. I would like to meet him someday."

Chinh brightened up slightly. "I'll try to get him to visit America. He's stubborn man but I think this time around he'll finally give in."

"I hope he does."

John's eyes were lost. He stared off in a distance where the silhouette of newly married couple walked hand in hand. Expiration date of this love he wondered till death do us apart was the one Metilda and I had vowed for.

Chapter 18

The day of the seventh kiss was a bright Monday morning. Metilda's skin looked almost translucent as John leaned at the porch steps to kiss her cheek.

Louis's cheeks were growing rosier by the day. He gleamed at his parents, a joy Metilda always longed to see in his eyes.

As John pulled away, his heart grew heavy. He turned his back toward them and started walking towards his1998 Mercedes.

I'm just going for work. He chanted inside his mind. Why is my heart so heavy? Why do I feel like something is missing? Why is my conscious killing me?

He turned around for a moment.

Sunlight danced off their fair skins. Metilda wore a lavender colored dress. Louis stood still next to his mommy, waiting for the arrival of the school bus. The wind tousled few strands of Metilda's hair. She caught John's gaze and smiled, a reassuring smile.

John took a deep breath. He knew everything was going to be okay. Louis and Metilda would be home when he returned.

The eighth kiss took place when John came to pick Louis up from school. It was a short peck on the lips as Metilda quickly pulled away. John had wanted to kiss her longer.

Louis once again was overjoyed. They met James mother and father, who very sweetly kissed their son, James.

Louis looked up his parents. The small eyes alight with joy.

On the other hand, John and Metilda's eyes couldn't have been sadder.

Honey colored eyes mourned for what was about to come while wild green ones mourned the fickle nature of time.

On the ninth kiss, sitting in the front-lawn, John had kissed Metilda. This time she didn't pull away.

She let him kiss her. They pulled away moments later when little Louis of five fell from his bicycle.

"I'm okay, mommy, daddy." He smiled at them. There was a scratch on his knee and Metilda panicked. John had to wind his arm around her to calm her down.

Her skin was a feverish red and so were eyes. John wondered if he could ever leave them alone. The worry would eat up his inside. Had Louis gotten to school on time? Was he alright? Had Metilda eaten? She often forgot to eat when she worked on her articles. He had to force her to drink some soup or chew on some bread.

She had grown so slim over the past months. Was it because he wasn't there to take care of her?

John's lips brushed against Metilda's head. The stars had risen. On the king-sized bed, a sleepy Louis sat awake in between his parents. He held both their hands tightly together.

"I love you. Mommy, daddy. Louis loves you."

With a peaceful smile, the little boy fell asleep, next to the warm, stiff bodies of his parents. A tear slipped out John's eyes. Did he really deserve his son's love?

Metilda didn't look his way. She stayed quite. Still. Frozen in time.

John was definitely not ready to let go. Metilda definitely couldn't hold on any longer.

The eleventh day came faster than John had expected. He stood in-front of the mirror in his bathroom. His heart beating insanely fast. Dread, fear, anxiety was all he could feel at the moment.

Just one more day. Metilda would no longer be in his life. His mornings would no longer hold those small joys, Louis's giggles, Metilda's soft laughs, the sound of Metilda singing to herself as she made breakfast, Louis's grumpy mood when he woke for school, the breakfast conversations he and Metilda held, Louis asking for help to tie his shoes, Metilda's flustered smile whenever John came into the kitchen.

John shook his head and buttoned up his vest.

When he arrived in the dining room, Metilda stood alone, looking out the window. Without giving it a second thought, John walked to where she stood.

He pulled her arm, cupped her face, and gave her the most passionate, loving kiss a man could ever give to a women. Metilda's eyes widened. She could have pushed him away but she didn't. Maybe she too felt the sadness he was feeling.

When their lips parted, John knew what he had to do.

He ran a tender hand across her jaw.

"Wait for me to come home."

Chapter 19

When John stood in front of the sturdy, burgundy door, his blood pressure soared, as though he had been approached by a drunk bull. John was about to knock on the door. It was six in the evening. He had to get home to Metilda.

But he retracted his hand a second later, his knuckles had barely touched the door. As he waited for Jannet to open the door, the moment she confessed her feelings for him flashed in-front of his eyes.

"I've been getting all these signs that you might like me." Jannet whispered bleary-eyed. She was drunk, not enough to lose control. She walked on her own and knew well enough what she was saying.

It was another party gone wrong. She was a broken hearted woman who always wore a strong face. He was a tired man who had nowhere to go.

John didn't say anything. He honestly didn't know what to say. They walked along the cold sidewalk for few minutes.

Jannet stopped walking.

John turned around.

Blue eyes blinking with tears took him in. John stiffly held out his blazer. "Are you cold?"

"A coat won't help with that." She sniffed.

It was strange for him to see her like that, to see the woman who barked orders at juniors, who didn't flinch once before pulling out her gun, who stood still in the face of danger, to see her crying. It was really strange.

"What's wrong?"

"I can't explain it."

She wore a gold sequined dress. Jannet was a stunning woman but John never really found any woman beautiful after Metilda. Not because Metilda was the most beautiful women alive but rather because she was so close to his soul. She was part of him, a part no human could ever replace.

He stared at her. The city lights blinked. Cars flew by. Wind rustled in between the empty spaces.

"Do you?" She whispered. Tears frozen on cheeks. Ice blue eyes held his captive.

"Do I what?" John stood still, a coward who refused to head to the warning sirens.

The city was alive yet dead. There were lights but there were no humans. Just two lost soul wandering on a rusted path. Yet the city pulsed, in the sound of tires hitting the gravel, in the distant sound of drunk teenagers muttering profanities. It was throbbing. Houston was watching. It was watching them make mistakes.

"Do you understand what I'm going through?"

He blinked once, twice. "No."

"I don't want to be the home wreaker. I'm not that kind."

"You cannot wreak what is already broken."

Something sparked inside her mellow eyes. John should have quenched the fire right then but his lonely heart wasn't listening. He needed someone and it was wrong. What is the use of morality that cannot be used? What is the use of noble values when not applied?

She took tentative steps towards. Stunning as she was, each step seemed as though it had been hit by lightning.

She held his jaw and kissed him.

And he kissed her back but as he did he saw a pair of honey eyes disappearing from his sight.

"Metilda"

John lowered his gaze to the doormat. Welcome.

This was it. This was goodbye.

Jannet opened the door a minute later. His heart felt heavy. The guilt has already begun eating him alive. She grinned at him, wearing another golden dress. She twirled in her spot. Her happiness, which he was about to shatter in a minute, made her face glow.

His head thrummed. A weight so heavy lay on his shoulders that they ached. So this is what hell felt like?

"...you came right on time. The New Year's party will start in half an hour or so we have plenty of time to get ready. Oh, this year is going to be great."

"Jannet." John sighed. He had to do this. This couldn't go on any longer. Regardless of Metilda, he couldn't lead Jannet on like this.

"Ah, why aren't you dressed?" She placed her hands on his chest, her finger ran along the collar of his shirt. "Not that you don't look dashing but John this is the biggest party of the year. At-least make an effort."

"Jannet!" He spoke a bit louder. It was loud enough to make Jannet jump back in surprise. Her blue eyes wide.

"What's wrong?"

"I can't do us anymore."

She looked at him. It was like she was looking at him for the very first time. Her mind understood the signs long before heart had started accepting them.

He wasn't the broken man anymore. There he stood tall and strong. He was being truthful for the very first time, to himself and to her.

"From our first kiss, it wasn't me who kissed you ever. It was the loneliness inside me. Throughout this entire relationship, I was never there. It was a man I don't know. A man who had been hiding from his demons. I was being a coward. Jannet, I'm sorry. I'm sorry for the mess I've made. I'm sorry for hurting you,"

She smiled and sighed. "She's back, isn't she?'

"What?"

"She's back in your heart. Your wife"

"To be honest, she never left."

Jannet bit her bottom lip. She wouldn't cry, she knew. "Good Luck then. I had a nice time with you."

John was slightly taken aback. "That's it. You're not going to beat me up or anything."

"Do you want me to?" She laughed, curly strands of hair bounced her off shoulders. "I'm not a child, John. I saw the signs from miles away. Twenty-seven years old and I've dated plenty guys to know when they're interested."

"Then why? If you knew. Why hurt yourself?"

She smiled, again-vainly. "Just go."

He opened his mouth.

"John. Please."

"Take care."

She didn't reply.

John entered an empty, one story house. He collapsed on floor near the entrance. Metilda hadn't listened to him after all. He shouldn't have expected her to either.

He could really use a couple shots or more. Alcohol wasn't a good solution.

He knew what his problem was. Even though Jannet hadn't shown it, he had hurt her. He had hurt

Metilda too. He slammed his hand into the door. A loud crackle thundered through the house.

John didn't think this burden was ever going to leave his shoulders. Somehow, he had to find a way to live with it.

Metilda and Louis stepped inside. Louis had a cherry lollipop while Metilda wore an emotionless face. She looked exhausted. On the other hand, Louis looked like a bubble of energy.

"Mommy, mommy. I want to eat ice cream and soda."

"No. Come on, time for sleep. Tomorrow's a big day."

It was the day of the twelfth kiss.

"Why is tomorrow a 'big day'? Is everything gonna be big on big day? Like big mousy pancakes?"

"Louis." Metilda smiled, slightly. "I'll tuck you in–"

"I want to sleep between mommy and daddy." Adorable green eyes looked at her.

Metilda didn't know what to say.

There was sound coming from the garage. Louis perked up at the noise. "Daddy's home! Mommy, daddy's home!" He ran and half jumped through the hall to the back door.

"Daddy! Daddy!"

Metilda walked behind him, wearily. "Wait for me to come home" He had said. He hadn't even waited for her answer. She wasn't the same Metilda. He couldn't expect that from her. This Metilda didn't gave a damn about their old traditions.

She loved him, yes. She loved her son as well.

When she reached the garage, she found Louis hoping up and down, trying to catch John's attention who was punching a free-standing heavy bag. Sweat trickled down his bare chest and seeped into the waist band of his shorts. He was out of breath yet eyes in complete focus.

Metilda could feel anger crawling up her skin. John should be resting. His arms were still healing. Straining them would only cause muscle damage.

Louis moved closer to his father. Adamant on catching his attention. Metilda's senses sharpened. No, no. The heavy bag was swinging back and forth. John's wasn't in full control.

The bag was inches away from Louis's face and...

"LOUIS!" Metilda screamed on top of her lungs.

But she didn't need to scream. John had snapped out of his daze a second earlier. He swooped Louis off and the ground into his arms.

"Whoa there, buddy." He smiled indulgently at Louis. "That was a close call."

"Daddy." Louis wrapped his arms around John. Completely oblivious to the accident about to happen minutes ago. "Louis wants to sleep with mommy and daddy today. James says he sleeps with his mom and dad every day."

John stole a glance at Metilda's face. All color had left it. She looked paler than a ghost. "Okay." John kissed his forehead. "First tell daddy where you two were? I was missing you."

Louis shrugged his shoulder. "Mommy met with doctor. Louis likes him because he gave Louis a lollipop."

"You shouldn't like people so easily." John's gaze was focused on Metilda. "So is there some trouble? Are you okay?"

"He's my friend." And you don't need to worry about me Metilda wanted to add but Louis's smile made all words dissolve in her mouth.

"Oh, that's nice."

In reality, John wanted to say everything but nice. Was there a new guy in Metilda's life? He and the lawyer might have competition.

John lay awake in bed. Louis snored softly beside him while Metilda's slow breaths accompanied them. His mind roamed about Jannet and Metilda. How in the world was he going to ask for Metilda's forgiveness? Would she forgive him? Would she let him back into her life after all the destruction he had done?

John turned over and stared at Metilda's back. He thought she was sleeping that is until her cellphone buzzed. He could see the screen's light create a vague outline of her head. Who was she texting? That too, this late.

It was an hour later when Metilda finally closed her phone that John fell asleep.

CHAPTER 20

After work, John bought twelve sunflowers. The lady at the flower store smiled at him.

"They're just lovely." John grinned. "I hope she likes them."

"She will." The lady replied. "Good luck."

"Thank you!"

He skipped, half walked to his car. Today was the day. The day he would try to win Metilda back and tell her how much he loved her. He didn't care about her answer. He just had to try. Once. Twice. Thrice. Maybe as long as his breaths ran. Maybe as long as his heart kept beating, he would try to win his only love back.

A breathless John arrived at the doorsteps of his house. When he opened the door, he found Metilda and Louis dressed and ready to go out. She had her purse ready and Louis had his monkey bag.

"Daddy's home." Louis rushed to John and hugged his legs.

"Yah. I'm home." John said, confused. Where were they going? His eyes fell on the baggage behind Metilda.

Louis jumped back and sat on the piles of luggage. "Louis and mommy gonna live with Aunt Talihra. Like a sleepover! Louis loves Aunt Talihra!" The five year old child giggled loudly.

"I-I" The banquet of flowers slipped out of John's hands. "You're moving out?"

She held his eyes. Emotionless. Vacant. Dead.

"I've signed the papers. They're on the table."

"But you can't go." He exclaimed.

"Daddy." Louis shook his head, like a grown up reprimanding a child. "We going for few days. Louis and mommy will come back soon."

"Yah." Metilda smirked. Her lips crooked. "We'll be back."

John pulled her waist. "Please, don't go." He lowered his gaze till his lips were grazing hers. "Please."

He kissed her as a silent plea.

The twelfth kiss was a desperate man trying to win back his wife.

Louis gasped, loudly. Green eyes became blank. The color began fading from his face.

Metilda and John instantly pulled away. Metilda rushed to his side, her hands gripping the small, feeble fingers.

Louis was struggling for every ounce of air. His cheeks grew white, and his lips were tinted blue.

"Mommy," Louis spoke between strangled pieces of air. "Louis can't...(gasp) breathe ....Mommy...help."

On the twelfth day, little Louis of five breathed his final breath.

And all was clear, the twelfth kiss was a mother fighting for her son.

CHAPTER 21

[13 days prior]

On Tuesday, Louis's teacher, Mrs. Findley had called Metilda for a private meeting. In her overly clogged room, Metilda sat stiffly in the upholstered chair. Mrs. Findley, an old lady with grey streaked hair, looked over the piles of papers. For the past the half an hour, she had been trying to convince a very odd thing to Metilda.

"...all the signs point towards it." She said for the tenth time.

Metilda glared at Mrs. Findley. "He does not have dyslexia."

"Just think about it Mrs. Hamington. With me, he hasn't been picking up things like the other kids. I've had a special education teacher to help with Louis."

"But you're saying that only happens occasionally and that his learning abilities are usually perfectly normal."

"Which is strange, I agree. I think..."

Metilda had enough. She stood up, her palms pressed into the worn, ply table. "Mrs. Findley I appreciated your concern but I don't think your opinion matters in this case. I will have a doctor decided what is wrong with my son."

"I'm sure the doctor will agree with me."

Oh my, Metilda had urge to scarf down an axe down that woman's throat. She smiled sweetly at the teacher. "We'll see."

Later, Metilda wished the doctor had agreed with Mrs. Findley. Mark Bortsov, a young Russian neurosurgeon, and Bob Lee, a middle aged brain specialist, wore grave faces as they announced to Metilda that little Louis of five, who had barely seen enough life to know what was going on, had a tumor in his brain.

Dr. Lee, folded his hands together and shifted in his chair towards Metilda. He had a dull expression on his wrinkled, long face. "The good news is it's a benign tumor. The bad news is that it is in a portion of the brain that is nearly impossible to operate on."

"He's showing symptom for dyslexia... not a tumor," This seemed like a bad dream to Metilda. It were as though she was speaking to the doctor from the safety of a glass screen called reality.

"That's the funny thing with the tumors. They don't have a definite set of symptoms. Currently," Dr. Lee pointed to the series of CT scans placed on the light box. "The tumor is pushing against the region of the brain responsible for memory and speech."

"One second." Metilda placed a hand on her chest. She could hear Louis outside the doctor's room, laughing and giggling with the nurse. She looked over her shoulder and saw him through the oval window in the door, showing the nurse his arms filled with colorful stickers. The staff ooh and aahed clearly taken into the little boy's charm.

She turned her attention back to the doctor. "What's going to happen..."

Dr. Lee shared a look with Mark Bortsov who leaned against the wall near the door with a nonchalant expression. He shrugged his shoulders, as if not wanting to elaborate or say anything for that matter.

Dr. Lee sighed. "The tumor is exerting a lot of pressure on the medulla oblongata. In layman's term, that means your son could experience shortness of breath, irregular heart rhythm."

"Just cut the chase and tell her." Mark uncrossed his arms and stood close to Metilda's chair. She craned her neck to look up at him. He was a broody, young man with an unkempt stubble, disheveled hair, and deep hooded grey eyes.

He looked directly into Metilda's eyes. "Your son is going to die."

"MARK!" Dr. Lee got up from his chair. "Where are your bedside manners? That is no way to talk to a patient."

Mark didn't seem fazed. His gaze was still focused on Metilda. "I'm not going to sugarcoat it. The pressure that tumor is creating is unbelievable. If we don't operate, he will die."

Metilda looked at Dr. Lee and then at him. "But he said it's impossible to operate-"

"It's not impossible. It's just that the chances of your son's surviving the operation are really low."

Dr. Lee seemed to be getting more furious by the second. "We've already had this discussion Mark.

You're not taking the chances. You know this operation won't be successful."

"Now look who has forgotten their bedside manners." Mark muttered under his breath.

Metilda felt her head spin. This wasn't making any
sense. There was a deep cliff either way.

She felt a cold hand on her shoulder. Mark's grey
eyes were determined. "I can help. In fifteen days'
time, I will be ready to operate on your son. The
choice is yours. You either accept fate as it is or fight
it."

Dr. Lee stared hard at Mark. "You will regret this.
This will tarnish your reputation" Those were his
last words before he exited the room.

"I want to fight."

He smiled at her, a calm smile. It somehow managed to make her feel a-lot stronger and hopeful.

She gave his hand a firm shake. "Thank you Doctor."

He looked at Louis and tightened his hold on her
hand. "It's too early for that."

Metilda felt the sunlight burning through every
pore of her skin as she walked alongside her new
friend, Mark. He was a neurosurgeon in the chil-

dren's ward of St. Mary Hospital. His height rounded off close to Metilda's.

Over the past week while coming for Louis's checkup, they had grown close enough to share the burdens of their hearts. Mark was a good listener and an excellent observer. Metilda had told him about her expedition to make John the kind of father Louis always wanted.

Today, Metilda had left Louis with John. She thought that John deserved some lone time with his son. Coincidentally, Mark had messaged her around the same time, saying that he was off for dinner and would love it if she could accompany him.

Gently, Mark placed a hand on Metilda's back. "Does it still hurt?"

She closed her eyes and released a pained breath. They stood outside the Thai restaurant near Brooklyn lane. "It doesn't matter."

"It does. You're showing all signs for depression. Back ache, loss of appetite, weight loss, and you're constantly tired."

"I've been taking anti-depressants and pain killers."

Mark let his hand drop to the side. His eyes watched the honey-hued sun dip below the horizon.

The traffic around them buzzed with excitement as headlights and streetlights became livelier.

"If I may ask, you've been this way for how long?"

Metilda wasn't interested in talking about this. She rubbed her hands together. "For too long."

"You know life doesn't stop because you do."

"I know."

"My friend, she's a pretty good psychiatrist. You could check her out."

Metilda shook her head. "I will after Louis's operation. Right now, my mind won't focus on anything else."

"Understandable."

Mark and Metilda walked in silence for few minutes. Metilda's fingertips brushed against Mark long fingers. She quickly retracted her hand. Mark noticed this and placed a polite distance between their bodies.

When they approached Metilda's car in the parking lot, Mark took both her hands in his, unable to hold it in any longer.

"I will give my everything to save him." Metilda noticed how strong his grip was and how fiery his eyes looked when he said that. "But if I'm unable to."

His hold on her hands got firmer. "I won't expect you to forgive me."

It was a natural reaction as Metilda wrapped her arms around his shoulders. Because for a mother, nothing meant more than someone trying to save her child.

[Present]

Chaos. Noise. Lights. That was the situation when little Louis of five was brought to the ER. Dr. Mark Bortsov took one look at Louis's face and knew that he would have to operate immediately. He quickly barked orders to the staff.

"Put him on oxygen. Now!"

His grey eyes met Metilda's teary red ones. He held his hand up in a reassuring gesture and mouthed the words it'll be alright.

Metilda collapsed on the metal chairs outside the ER. Numb and frightened. She held her hands together in a prayer.

Seconds later, a dazed John returned from the reception.

"They said... something about a tumor and operation." One look at Metilda's somewhat calm yet tensed face. He knew that she had known all along. "What's going on?"

She opened her eyes. Her lips frozen mid-way through the prayer.

Chapter 22

There was bliss in pain. Metilda had found it. In the jarring, unsettling noise of the humans wailing and screaming around her. She found bliss. Quaint bliss. Her nerves were calm, the turmoil brewing inside her heart had settled. She had done all she could. To make the last thirteen days pleasant for Louis. His last wish of having a family like James had been fulfilled.

She didn't need to cry no-more. She didn't need to stress no-more. It was all out of her control now. May the stars are fall out of the sky or may the sky bend over to steal her son, she wouldn't question it. All she could do was pray, pray for that Almighty being to be kind and to grace a five year old's life.

"I surrender" She whispered. Her lips froze when another voice joined hers.

"What's going on?"

Wild green eyes stared at her, hard.

It was sign or she thought. The instant she had given herself up, the man had drifted so far from her, stood in-front of her.

Vulnerable and baffled.

He had the right to know after all he was the father.

"Louis... he... (cough)." Her voice was ragged, each breath seemed to lag a mile behind. "(cough)...has a tumor in his brain...it couldn't be operated on easily. He... our son, might not make it."

John made a strangled noise as he sunk onto the hospital floor. "You've known for how long?"

"Thirteen days."

Metilda chewed down on her lower lip to stifle the sob about to erupt.

The man who had always thought logically, who never fully heeded to emotions, who hid his scars so well, broke down. A hurricane of sadness, dejection, hatred fled him. John shook under the weight, the burden of the world lay on his shoulders.

He hated himself. He despised his existence.

Blurry eyes looked at his own empty hands. "What kind of father am I? Am I so bad that you had to hide all this from me? DAMN IT! I wanted get rid of my own blood and flesh but I never wanted him to... Why? Why?"

John slammed his hands into his chest. "Why? Why? This is all my fault."

Metilda kneeled down beside John and took his shaking shoulders in her hands. Not a single word escaped her lips as she wove her hands under his arms, holding them against her fragile body.

John closed his eyes.

He was a sinking ship and she was his shore that was the kind of desperation with which he clung to her.

Cool, moist air flittered in through the open window. Talihra sat beside Metilda, the warmth of her leg pressed against hers provided some comfort. Seconds had turned to minutes to hours, Metilda had lost count. John leaned against a distant wall. His eyes fixed on Metilda yet his mind wandered far away.

Jai, Talihra's husband, a short lean Indian man sat on the row chairs opposite to Metilda and Talihra. He was a kind man. The way he had reassured John was quite remarkable. He had only placed a hand on John's shoulder and said these words: "you cannot change what has happened. Accept the present and pull yourself together for your son. He could use every ounce of positivity at the moment."

For the first the time in four hours, Metilda looked up at John. He was as broken as she was. Maybe even more. He needed her. She needed him. He needed her to reassure him. She needed him to fight the demons.

She got up from her chair. The movement barely registering in her mind. John momentarily snapped out of the storm of chaotic thoughts. Before any another thought could pull her apart, she took hold of John's arm.

"I-I.." Her vision was blurred by tears. She began sobbing. "I-I'm sorry."

John wrapped his strong arms around her, holding her close to his chest. Metilda took a deep breath in, his scent lulling her mind into half-awake state.

"Our baby will be okay, right?"

John nodded, tightening his grip around her.

At the same moment, Dr. Mark came out of the operation theatre followed by his team. Metilda slipped from John's grasp as she rushed towards Mark.

Mark, his grey eyes looked more tired, his hair was more disordered than before. He gently caressed the back of Metilda's hand.

"The tumor was removed successfully."

Metilda breathed a sigh of relief. "Can I see him?"

"No, not yet. He hasn't regained consciousness..."

Mark's behavior seemed slightly off- Metilda noted.

"What's wrong?"

John stood behind Metilda. He held Mark's gaze. "Is my son okay?"

Mark glanced at his team and dismissed them before turning his attention back to the couple.

"We don't know."

In a flash, John's hands were gripping Mark's collar. He slammed Mark against the wall. All eyes in the hall were fixed upon them. The reception manager was about to call the police but Mark held up his hand, stopping her in the process.

"What do you mean by that?" John growled.

"Sir, please remove your hands."

When John's fingers didn't budge, Mark gripped his wrists and yanked his hands off. The man was strong, John had to give him that. His fist was about to collide with Mark's broody face when Metilda knocked John backward.

She held John's arm. "Let him talk. Please."

"Mark, what are talking about?"

Mark ran a hand across his jaw. "Until Louis regains consciousness, there is no telling anything. The damage caused by the removal of the tumor is unknown. The only logical guess I have is that since the tumor was so close to the motor coordination area that Louis may have difficulty in walking, maybe do doing simple things like eating. I can't say anything for sure. We have to wait till he wake up."

He patted Metilda's shoulder and walked away, leaving a broken man and a frazzled mother to fend for themselves.

CHAPTER 23

"D addy" was the first word Louis had said. John beamed at Metilda. He picked up his baby boy into his arms.

"Say it again." Louis giggled as he clasped John's ear. He had lost attention now.John looked at Metilda his eyes wide.

"Had he really said daddy? Had he really?"

Metilda nodded smiling.John had never felt happier in his life. He kissed Louis's cheeks. "I love you buddy,"

John reeked of winter, sadness, and despair. Every passerby would glance at his face, the haunting empty eyes of a defeated man. A shudder escaped the new ward boy. He wasn't used to seeing such pain, let alone experiencing it.

John didn't know what to do. Metilda was inside with the doctors. Louis had regained consciousness. They were accessing his condition. He could have gone with Metilda but he was scared. A coward everyone may call him. A worthless man who doesn't deserve an ounce love is what Talihra used to call him.

Talihra stood near the door with Jai standing behind her. They both looked worn with worry. Metilda's parents Dr. Harrison Wells and Mary Wells were sitting on the benches opposite to John's. They sat hand in hand. Dr. Wells gently caressed Mrs. Wells arm. This incident was as much as shock for them as it had been to John. After all, they loved their very grandson dearly.

Metilda came out followed by Mark. There was a willowy smile lighting her features. Mark gave Metilda a tight hug before leaving with his staff. John didn't miss the way Mark's hand lingered a second longer on her waist.

Metilda turned to face her family. "He's okay. He's asleep but he's okay" Tears brimming in her honeysuckle eyes. "He's alive. He's breathing and that's all that matters. Mark says that he has lost sensation in his left leg but his motor neurons are alright so he shouldn't have trouble walking. I ju-just can't believe he's okay..."

John zoned out as he watched the scene around him.

Talihra was the first to cheer out loud. Dr. Wells grinned from ear to ear. Mrs. Wells quietly bowed her head, thanking the universe for its kindness. Talihra lifted Metilda off the ground while Jai laughed at his wife's excitement.

John smiled. As he stood up, to walk to his Metilda, to home, to the universe, his star, his moon, his sun, his light, he stopped. On Metilda's hand that gripped Talihra's shoulder, their wedding ring no longer adorned it.

The past 12 days he had spent were with Louis's mother, not his wife. He had lost that woman a long time ago.

"Where's John?" Mrs. Wells asked her daughter.

Metilda shrugged her shoulder. They sat on chairs next to Louis bed, watching him snore softly. "I don't know."

"Mella, Is everything alright between you two?"

"No." Metilda wanted to focus on her son, not John. At the moment, she didn't even know what to feel.

Mrs. Wells didn't ask her anymore. Probably sensing Metilda's reluctance or perhaps she had something else on her mind.

"You know your father never told me that he loved me." Mrs. Wells stared out the window. The ember trees glowed in the setting sun's light.

This had caught Metilda attention. She turned to face her mother. "Really? You've been married for forty years. Dad has never said I love you.

Mrs. Wells nodded, smiling. "Not even once."

"Why? I mean how..."

"do I even know that he loves me?" She completed for her. Mrs. Wells resembled Metilda in many ways. The quirk of her eyebrow, the lightness of laugh, the gentleness of her speech.

"Harrison was never big on pretenses."

"Mom but still....how hard is it to say I love you. Three words, really?"

"Just as easy it is to say let's get divorced."

Metilda averted her gaze. "Who told you?"

Mrs. Wells smiled, a secretive smile. "When I had my first heart attack, after the operation, my chest began bleeding profusely. You know how much your father fears the sight blood. Yet he was the one who screamed for the doctors. He was the one who held my hand while the nurse cleaned me up. No amount of I love you could compare to the love I felt then."

"He got distracted." She stroked her daughter's hair. "When you fell asleep last night, he was the one who brought pillows for you to rest your head on. This morning, he was the one who had brought breakfast. I don't think that man has eaten anything in the past twenty-four hours yet he makes sure you are fed. If that isn't love, my dear, I don't know what is."

Chapter 24

The wind chimes tinkered. Gently. Ever so beautifully. The trees, sunflowers glowed in the early morning sunlight. John stood in the back porch. His head resting on the wooden pillar. He inhaled deeply.

The dusk of dawn singled a new beginning. Perhaps a beginning without him.

He looked at his empty hands. The gruff skin that stubbornly clung to his bones and how once upon a time, a hand perfectly enveloped his.

"John" Metilda running around their small garden. "No, you wouldn't dare." She was laughing, loudly as though the world had gifted her every ounce of happiness. .

John grinned, his hands dripping with paint. "I would."

"No." She breathlessly huffed, hiding behind the oak tree. "The baby doesn't approve."

"I'm sure our baby doesn't mind daddy giving mommy a little color."

"JOHN!" Before Metilda had the chance to react, John had pressed his hands against her face.

She pouted at him. "Look at what you've done. Happy now?"

John laughed. "Very happy!"

A moment later she joined him.

John could still hear their laughter as he stood under the slanting roof. It echoed off the walls. On the oak tree's trunk, the paint splatters still adorned it. The garden had soaked in their moments. It still held them in its safety even when he had forgotten them.

John wandered aimlessly through their house. He stopped at Metilda's room. It used be the spare guest room. She had taken it up when John had spilled beans about Jannet.

He ran his hands along the bedspread. The flower designs reminded him of the time he and Metilda went to shop for household items and how she had wanted floral prints on everything -from cookware to the drapery.

"Flowers, flowers." She swung their adjoined hands back and forth. "They lose themselves for others. It's like they have a sense of sacrifice. Their petals wither away once they turn into fruits. Beauty gives way for love."

"That doesn't make any sense."

"Not everything has to."

John smiled to himself.

He made his way to the living room. His eyes taking in everything yet leaving everything. Tears dripped from his face.

He loved her. He loved her. He love them, his son and his wife.

After one final glance, John picked up his bags and left. The remaining memories in the house beckoning him to return but he held it all in and ignored the call of his heart.

"Louis is a little bunny. Bunnies like to hop-hop and..."

Louis jumped up and down on the hospital's bed, giggling as he went up. The nurse trying to ease him back down so she could administer the medicines.

"Louis sit back down. Louis!"

Metilda was in a middle of a fit when Mark entered the room. He looked broodier than ever. Black strands of hair strewn carelessly across his forehead.

"Hey Louis! All good?" Mark instantly smiled.

Whenever Mark saw kids, his usual broody self-changed into something cheery. He felt pretty happy when he talked to Metilda as well who looked absolutely beautiful, even in her dismantled state, with hair falling out of her bun, tired lines across her forehead.

"Louis is a bunny. With cute lil'ears and a big nose." Louis pointedly scrunched his noise. "See Louis is a bunny."

Mark placed a reassuring hand on Metilda's shoulder. "He's okay. Metilda. We've got him."

She closed her eyes for a moment and when she opened them, she seemed more relaxed.

"Hey bunny." Metilda smiled at Louis. A blue cap was wrapped around his head. "If you don't come back down then mommy won't take you to the carnival."

Louis perked up at the mention of carnival.

"Mhm, pink cotton candy and gummy bears."

Metilda rolled her eyes at Mark's childlike tone but laughed nevertheless.

"Okay. Louis will eat medicine." He plopped back down on the bed and held his mouth wide open. Metilda helped him drink the cap filled with a brown colored liquid. Louis made a gagging face before swallowing the liquid.

"Louis go to carnival with mommy and daddy." He yawned, nestled his head against the stuffed bunny with two buttons for eyes. "Mommy, daddy, and Louis go the..."

He dozed into sleep. Metilda sighed.

"Can I have word with you?" Mark whispered in her ear.

She looked at him, confused. "Of-course.

Mark and Metilda sat outside in the hospital's garden. The grass was being mowed in a distance. Few couples were strolling along the concrete fountain circle.

The sun was bright in the sky. The winds were gentle, the birds were chirping. Few strands of hair flew across Metilda's face. Mark leaned forward and tucked them behind her ear. Metilda felt wry at the action.

"There's something I have been meaning to ask you."

Something twisted inside her gut. A feeling she knew quite well. The temperature of her skin rose few notches.

Mark bent down on his knees and looked up at her.

"Will you marry me?"

A velvet box lay in his palm in which shone a gold band.

CHAPTER 25

Metilda felt the rush of the wind caressing her skin, the bellowing sound of the lawn mower. Her eyes, of clear honey, watched Mark with bafflement.

He sat on his knee, the stethoscope hanging around his neck, his hair in an entangled mess. His grey eyes accessed her carefully, a calm reflection on his features.

He didn't look like a man who was proposing to the love of his life. His relaxed demeanor gave it away.

Metilda remembered the time John has proposed. The way his hands shook, sweat trickled down his forehead, and how it looked like his life depended on her answer.

"Is this some kind of joke?" Metilda spoke through gritted teeth. "I mean, Mark... we're nothing of that sorts."

Mark smiled and rose to his feet. He tucked the velvet case carefully in his pocket. "That's what I thought too"

"What do you mean?"

Mark settled down next to Metilda. "The ring I actually bought for my girlfriend. I'm going propose to her tonight."

Metilda looked even more confused than before. She drew her eyebrows together. "Are you-"

He held up his hand. Silencing her. "John came to my cabin yesterday. He has something very interesting to say."

There was a knock on Mark's door. He had just fallen asleep in the doctor's lounge. Couldn't they leave him alone for one second? The man needed at-least few hours of sleep.

When Mark reached the door, he found John standing there. For a moment, he feared for his life. What if he was here to arrest him? Or even worse, kill him.

But one look at John's face, erased all of Mark's fears.

He had the face of a defeated man.

"He wanted me to take care of you. He thinks we have something going on. I have no idea where he got this idea from."

Metilda gripped the golden band hanging around her neck from a thin silver chain. After signing the divorce papers, she no longer had a reason wear it but she couldn't let it go.

A sinking feeling entered Metilda's heart. What could he possibly be thinking? She tried assuring herself, desperately, as a lost sailor trying to reach for shore.

When Mark noticed the tensed look on Metilda's face, he placed a hand on her shoulder. "I swear I've never seen you in that way. You and Louis made me so happy. At times, I thought of you as my own family. But Metilda, I'm sorry if I've caused a rift between John and you."

Metilda shook her head. "It's not that, Mark. I'm just worried." She looked at Mark's grey eyes. For a moment, she saw wild green brimming with tears fill her vision. She blinked once, twice. "John isn't the kind of man who would bend his pride like that. He would rather die."

"Maybe you don't know him well enough."

She smiled. "Ten years have fallen short, I suppose."

Talihra was a bustle of activity when she arrived at the hospital. She carried plastic containers stuffed with sandwiches and a pitcher filled with warm tea.

She set it all on the table in hospital canteen.

"You won't believe what I saw."

Metilda unwrapped a cucumber sandwich and began nibbling on it. "Okay."

Talihra let out an exaggerated sigh. "Ah, come on! Show more excitement! This news will blow your mind away."

"Talihra, please. I'm not in the mood."

The excitement drained from Talihra's face. She took a seat across Metilda and poured Metilda a cup of herbal tea. Steam rose in the air, Metilda deeply inhaled it, savoring every sip.

"What did you see?" Metilda tried appearing interested for Talihra's sake.

It worked apparently as Talihra reverted back to her excited self. "I went to that new store down

Brooklyn lane and guess who I saw intensely making out."

"Who?"

"Jannet and-"

"John" Metilda completed wearily for her. Suddenly, she felt sick till her stomach.

"No," Talihra shook her head. "It was some chubby guy called Sam. I think she's cheating on John. Serves him right, doesn't it?"

Metilda didn't respond and instead reached for cellphone. She dialed John's number.

Talihra looked at her weird. "Who are you calling?"

"John. He hasn't visited us since yesterday. I hope he's okay."

"Are you serious? You can't possibly still care for that man."

"I've never stopped caring, Talihra and I never will." Metilda set her cellphone down. A panicked expression on her face. "I think something's wrong. He isn't picking up his phone."

"He rarely ever did."

"No. You won't understand." Metilda rose from her chair. Her heart beating insanely fast. A feeling inside her chest told that John had taken a drastic step.

"Where are you going?" Talihra yelled after Metil-da.

"To find John. I need to see him."

Talihra's eyes widened. "You can't be serious. He cheated on you. You can't be thinking of giving him another chance to hurt you."

She held her gaze. Steady and calm. "It doesn't matter when you realize that I wasn't the only one hurting in this relation."

Heels and shoes clicked on the limonium floors. Smell of perfume, rotting meat, sweat encircled the small train station. John sat near the ticket counter. He had spent his night siting here. Watching people pass him by. Two hours till the train for Boston would arrive. Two hours till his life here would fade into a mark in his memory.

He heaved a pained sigh, bags lying next his legs.

I don't want to leave. He stared at the large digital clock.

He closed his eyes.

Aunt Rein was stroked his hair. "You promised me, John. You would win Metilda back no matter what it takes. You promised to keep trying till your breaths ran short."

"She's out of my reach now. Mark..."

"How do you know, dear boy, you've made as-
sumptions and how could you leave your son like
that. At-least say goodbye to him."

John opened his eyes. "Louis."

Metilda was worn to the bone. She had searched
everywhere from their house to John's office, he was
no-where to be found. Defeated, she returned to the
hospital.

There was noise coming from the Louis's room,
laughing noises. A familiar sound made Metilda's
heart halt. John's laugh. It was the most pleasant
sound to her ears.

She rushed inside to find Louis riding on John's
back. The joy in Metilda's eyes as she watched John
and Louis cannot be comprehended in words. This
is the point of the story where my words won't be
enough to describe all that is taking place. Stand
in a crowd of strangers, the moment a familiar face
emerges among the unknown, the peace you feel
cannot be written about.

Louis tightly hugged John's neck. "Faster, daddy,
faster." His arms spread wide as though he were a
bird soaring the infinite skies.

John's gaze was captured by Metilda. He drew in a sharp piece of air. This was going to be so much harder.

In the crowd of patients and nurses, no-one noticed as Metilda's hand traced John's wrist. They stood outside Louis's room. Their angel was fast asleep.

"Where are you going?"

John's eyes were hesitant and didn't have the courage to meet hers. "To Jannet."

"Jannet who?"

John didn't reply. He didn't know how to.

"Jannet, the woman, you broke up with two days ago because you realized you loved your wife."

John finally looked at Metilda. The evening sun cast an ember glow on her skin. She was truly beautiful. "How do you know?"

Metilda smiled to herself. "She called to see if Louis was alright. It's strange. But I never hated her. Even when she took away the most important person in my life." John noticed how Metilda's grip was becoming stronger, how the smile on her lips was growing, how she was closing the distance between their bodies. She carefully entwined their fingers together. "I'm glad that she did because I would have never realized my mistake and you would have never told me."

John was on the verge of tears.

"Please don't." He told her. "Please don't. I've wronged you in so many ways. Metilda, I don't have the guts to apologize. You've been through the hell because of me. I don't deserve your forgiveness."

"No, you don't." She whispered. Her hands now rested on his arms. "You deserve my love."

"You'll be disgusted with me if you knew the real reason for everything I did. I dated Jannet because I wanted your attention. I wanted to hurt you like I was hurting. I wanted you to suffer."

"No, John. It wasn't you that wanted all of that. It was your ego." She brought her hands to his face. Few tears trailed on John's sharp Jaw, Metilda's feeble fingers brushed them away. "John, we have to accept change. I had Louis to take care of. We can't always be madly in love, now can we?"

"I know."

"Everyone thinks I was the only hurt, I was the victim. But I know you've gotten through pain more than I have. Every time you yelled at me, I saw the guilt in your eyes." At this point, a sob escaped John's mouth. "I saw you stay awake for every night that we fought. I saw you linger by my room when I was pretending to be asleep."

Metilda took a deep breath in. "I forgive you, John. Please forgive yourself as well."

John nodded and wrapped his arms around Metilda. Two bodies merged into one. The world drifted past them as their hearts became whole once again.

I want to say that they lived happily ever after but that would be a lie. They faced many more storms after that day but they faced them together. In each other's companion, they found bliss. When the world would tire them, peace would be painted by the quiet talks they shared.

And so, John and Metilda lived happily together after.

Chapter 26

Summer 1999

"Brady nicked my wallet." John brushed his leather jacket and worn jean trousers. There was dust on them, he had clearly just gotten out of a fight. His black hair was slicked to one side, slightly edging over his wild green eyes. It was clear to Metilda that he was going for Rocky Balboa look.

She laughed, her ruby lips curled upwards. "What a terrible excuse for a roommate."

"Hey!" John stood taller. A bit offended. "I won't hear anything against my best-friend. Even though he can be a scoundrel at times-he's the best I've got."

"I'll go grab my purse." Metilda rolled her eyes. She secretly liked that about John. He was faithful to his friends and those he loved.

Her hands reached for brass handle to her dorm room when John fingers found hers. He smelt strongly of some male musk. Valentio, Metilda concluded, was her favorite smell. His face was freshly shaven. He had really made an effort to impress her.

A scarlet red color fled her face when she realized one of girls from the lower grade was watching them and John quickly withdrew his fingers.

"It's our first date." John stared hard at his polished black shoes as though they were far more interesting than the blushing girl standing at the steps of a sorority house.

"I know, Mr. Jack Reacher."

"Well, the lady should never pay on the first date."

Metilda eyebrow shot a mile in the air. "Is there a rule against it?"

"No, well..." John cleared his throat awkwardly. "I wanted to do this right... I didn't mean that you aren't capable of taking me out...I'm not doubting you. Women are great, beautiful wondrous creatures but I-I"

She sighed. "We're humans. Just like you men are. John, shake yourself out of this stage fright. We were friends before confessing. As a matter of fact, we still are."

"Sorry." John grinned sheepishly. "I just can't believe you said yes."

Metilda felt her cheeks strain into a grin, mirroring John's. She was so gone.

"My friend, Liz, the photographer has gone out to take some wedding pictures."

John looked at her, unsure. "Okay."

"I think the venue was the Lilac Garden, you know the park next to South Avenue. We could crash it. I mean not, crash crash it but like for free food. What do you say?"

John looked tempted but still unsure. "Don't you think they'll mind?"

"Nah. They're quite rich" Metilda linked her arm with John, well-aware of her classmates peeking through the blinds. She could almost hear their dreamy sighs as John hesitatingly put his hand on her small back.

"Let's go then."

Summer 2015

There was hesitation in John's eyes. Every day, every hour, every second, and with every breath he took, there was hesitation in the moments he spent with Metilda. She wasn't the same woman he had loved at the blossom of youth. The fading of years had changed her. Or maybe it was his betrayal.

Because this woman, who once was confident, brave, and strong, was now trying to salvage the little self-respect she had. She would smile, laugh with John, but her eyes, always guarded, her response always short, and less warm than what it used to be.

Ninety days had passed since Louis was discharged from the hospital. The little angel had gone to a field trip with school. Though Metilda was against it, Louis had begged his parents until they gave in.

John wanted to seize this opportunity to take Metilda out for a date.

He stood at the doorway of her room. She sat at the worn maple desk, in her separate room from John. She hadn't moved into their bedroom and John didn't ask her why.

He straightened his posture, his hands clammy like from the time of their first date. The soothing melody of her fingers hitting the keyboard halted when John knocked the door.

She turned around slightly, blinking a couple times as though she had lost her train of thoughts.

"Do you need something John?" Her voice was a calm resembling a tropical summer wind.

"Um...not really." He didn't dare to set a foot inside her room. The idea intimidated him for he no longer knew how she would react. Would she push him out or pull him closer? "Are going to be free in the evening?"

Metilda started at the clock, biting on her lower lip. She did that when she was nervous or excited. "I have therapy in the evening. So I should be free around eight." Then a slow smirk slid on her lips. It reminded John of the young Metilda. "Planning to take me on a date, Johnny boy."

John let out a nervous laugh. "Something like that."

Metilda watched him for a moment. A strange silence settled between them. It wasn't suffocating nor was it comforting. It was like an empty void that was begging to be filled. John couldn't help noticing the slight amount of color returning to her cheeks.

She was slowly gaining weight and it was for the better.

"I should finish this article." Metilda said. Breaking the silence, painfully.

John nodded. He was about to leave. "Metilda."

"Yes, John."

"I love you." Surprise flickered upon her face, as an open flame under the early spring rain. Her honey eyes, that reminded John a fleeting winter afternoon, were wide.

John wanted her to say the words out loud. Metilda's lips parted, she was about to say something, but her voice abandoned her midway.

It took her moment to find her voice.

When she did, John's chest thudded painfully. "I do too."

The hesitation in her voice was something John would never forget. It wasn't because she was unsure of her love for him, it was because she was scared of hurt, of letting him know how much he meant to her. Because once upon a time, Metilda had given everything to John and he had thrown it all away.

John smiled, not bitterly, but in remorse.

Forgiveness was more easily given than faith, he finally concluded.

CHAPTER 27

S ummer 1999

It was the most beautiful summer of John's life. His twenty-first summer where every petal was in its full glory. Like stars, falling from the heaven, soft-butter like flowers of the pink crape myrtle fell into Metilda's hair.

John was dark, at times talkative, sometimes awkward, and most times a star.

Metilda was quiet, shy, sometimes kind, sometimes understanding, and always sincere.

They sat under a tree, in the park, watching the wedding procession from a little distance away. The wedding was so beautiful that Metilda didn't have the guts to intrude. It felt wrong to do so.

So John and Metilda sat, a polite distance between their bodies, to watch everything unfold.

"Have you ever been in love?" John asked, from the corner of his eye he saw Metilda stiffen. The answer was clear as daylight.

"Yes." She bit her lower lip, which was trembling. "I really loved him." Her gaze was averted, it didn't meet his.

"What happened?"

"Sometimes," She held up her hand. And a moment later she joined it with her other hand, an inch of air separating them. "One person can't break all the walls. I tried really hard to get to him. Relentlessly, I kept trying and trying to make him see, to make him understand that he could trust me."

Metilda closed her eyes, taking a deep breath. "You can't break the barrier unless the other person wants you to and he didn't want me. Which really hurt. It hurt so bad. Eventually, I became just like him until you came along..."

John want to weave his fingers through her hand. But it would be too direct, maybe it was too early. Instead, he opted to lean into the tree's rough bark.

"They keep pushing you away because they want you to try harder and when you leave, it devastates them. I saw it in your eyes Metilda. Every time you pushed me away or ignored me for days, your hands would shake whenever you saw me. It's hard to love again, once it's been lost. That what happened to me when I lost my parents. Aunt Rein was the one who put up with my mood swings. One day she forgot to call me, and Metilda I had never felt so scared in my life. I thought what if she gave up on me. What will I do then?"

"I'm glad that you didn't." Metilda whispered. The violinist was playing a broken melody, by the bench. It was his first time attempting the song. She took a deep breath. "I'm glad that you didn't give up on me."

John smiled slightly, before nodding. Black strands of hair strewn carelessly across his forehead. The melody of the violinist was growing stronger.

"Have you ever been in love?" Metilda finally asked, unable to keep it in.

"You mean before you, no. not really. I've liked girls but love-"

The colors of summer rushed to Metilda's face. The simmering sun, the hot humid air, the balminess of the wind must have done its magic. Because John had never seen her look so red.

"Are you okay, Metilda?"

She stopped mid-way a nod. "You just said- I-. John." It was clear, she was a mess.

"I've told you before, Mel. I love you."

It was the first time John had directly said those words to her. Their very first I love you. Metilda was about to open her mouth to reply, but John pressed a hand to her lips. A very bold move.

"It's okay. You don't have to say it. Not until you're sure."

Summer 2015

John stood outside the rehab center. His heart beating a mile a minute. Metilda walked out five minutes later, simply dressed in a navy blue skirt and white blouse.

John, who was wearing a tight tuxedo, had made reservations at some fancy restaurant. Metilda frowned the instant she caught his eyes, the woman around her were giggling at John like no tomorrow.

"John."

"Mel." Her heart gave a slight squeeze. It had been awhile since he had last called her Mel.

He was dressed in his finest clothes. A muffler in the left pocket of his coat, a steely grey tie loosely hanging from the collar. Sleek strands of hair combed to one side, his face freshly shaved.

Metilda didn't want this memory resurface but it did.

She sat near the windowsill, of the living room, working on a pending article. The early morning sunlight streaming through the window. It was hard for her to wake up every morning, even when her mind was too numb to think, to command her body to move, to smile when she saw her son. It was hard.

John emerged from his room. Metilda scanned what he was wearing. Nicely polished shoes, a brand new coat and shirt, an expensive watch in his left hand. He was certainly dressed to impress. No, not her. To impress Jannet.

As he drifted away, Metilda realized he wasn't wearing her favorite scent anymore. It was a new smell.

It should have hurt. Maybe a little. Because as John passed by her, he didn't even glance her way. But it didn't. Metilda was too numb to care anymore.

"How was therapy?" John asked, closing the distance between them in long strides. He stopped at a polite distance apart.

Metilda smiled at him. "It was good." He hated how vague her answers were these days. He wished she would tell him more things. "I've learned a-lot of things about myself."

"Like what?"

John and Metilda advanced towards his car. It was parked few feet away from where they stood.

"John." Metilda abruptly stopped walking when her fingers brushed against his leg.

"I'm listening." He turned to face her.

"I appreciate the efforts you're making but I'm not ready. It doesn't feel right. I'm sorry. I know I've for-given you but it feels like we're rushing into things. I'm scared that it might crash and burn again."

It was the most Metilda had said in the past few days. John took a deep breath, the light smile on his lips seemed to be transfixed.

"We can be friends for the time being. As long as you're with me, you know Metilda I'm fine with being just friends for the rest our life."

All breaths were caught in her throat. She smirked. "Still smooth as ever, old man." She nudged her shoulder with him.

John frowned at her. "I'm not old. Not from any angle.'

"Sure, you're not."

"Hey. This isn't fair."

"Life isn't fair."

"True."

"So Johnny boy," Metilda placed a hand on her hip, while John leaned against the car's frame. "Where do you plan to take me tonight?"

John's smile grew fonder and wider. "To the golden old days."

Summer 1999

Metilda was dancing a little distance ahead of him, the cotton sun dress she wore fluttered in the air, her cheeks were stained a rosy pink as John's wild green eyes followed her.

They were in his aunt's backyard. She was out of the city for an interstate chess competition, leaving the house to his care. Metilda, bare footed, splashed in the mud puddles, leaving footprints all over the gravel.

John would have to clean it later but he honestly didn't mind. Seeing her happy made him so happy. A couple of hours of scrubbing would be worth it.

Metilda walked back to John, where he stood, leaning against the maple tree trunk.

"You know," She dragged the word. "When a boy brings a girl to an empty house, he usually has something on his mind."

John flushed red. Metilda had a hard time believing that he was the same boy who was the life of a party, confident and bold. He was everything but such when with her.

"I promise, I wasn't thinking anything like that."

Metilda narrowed her eyes at him and surveyed him carefully, her index finger tapping the tip of her chin. "I believe you."

She spun to the other side and John released a sigh of relief.

Then she looked over her shoulder, a twinkle of mischief in her eyes. "But that doesn't mean I wasn't thinking about it."

Summer 2015

Metilda bit her lower lip. Amusement clear as day in her eyes. "John, you must be really desperate to bring me here."

She stood at the doorstep of his dead aunt's house.

John scratched the back of head, smiling sheepishly. "Desperate, maybe a little bit but that's not what I had in mind."

Metilda rolled her eyes. "I'm leaving."

"What? No. Wait!" John raced after Metilda as she trudged ahead. He reached forward to grab her hand which she slapped away.

"Don't touch me."

"Metilda."

John sighed. He had really cut himself a slice of trouble now. There was only one way to convince her. John could already feel himself going hot and red from embarrassment.

Epilogue

Summer 1999

They sat in John's old room at his aunt's house. By the window, watching the world drift by, the sky pale into maroons, velvety blues. Their legs a tangled mess, their hearts soaring freely as those proud sparrows. Metilda leaned into his chest, breathing deeply, she was half-asleep. There was a content smile on her lips.

John's fingers lingered on her forehead, tucking the stray strands of hair behind her ear. He sighed, his head resting on the cold glass pane.

"Metilda?"

"Mhm," She murmured, snuggling closer to him.

"I don't want to lose you, ever."

She peeked through almost closed eyelids. "You won't."

"How can you be so sure?"

He shifted slightly, her head firmly pressed above his heart. "Because I love you." It was her confession. She even as she said it causally, her voice barely above a whisper, her breaths steady- the scarlet color of her cheeks gave away her true feelings.

John pulled her closer. "I've lost too many people in my life. At times, I have to remind myself that you'll be there tomorrow, the day after that. Every moment we spend together feels like our last." He held her hand, observing how smaller it was from his, almost like a doll. "My older brother and I, we used to be such good friends. He was my best-friend. But as time moved on, he's become so estranged from me. We barely see each other. I hope that doesn't happen to us. You know, Metilda, I hope that kind of bitterness never enters our hearts."

She gripped his hand, tightly, looking up into his green eyes, she smiled. "It won't happen to us. I promise."

"What if it does?"

She pointed at the sky, where a flock of bright blue jays flew high in the sky. "They're amazing, aren't they? No-one teaches them the way, but they still know it." Light, honey colored eyes met his. "A bird always finds its way home and John, you're my home."

The wind gently caressed their skins, her hair flew haphazardly, nestling against her warm bosom.

"You know when people say its small world,"

He nodded, urging her to go on.

"What they don't realize is that the world isn't a small place. It's their hearts finding the way to one another. Just as birds, we too have that instinct. Just as birds, for whom a place isn't a home, but the birds that fly with them."

"If I drift away." John whispered. "Promise me, you'll find me again."

"I will. Until my very last breath." She smiled. "If I'm ever far away, just sing me a song and I promise I'll come back."

"You will?"

"There's no doubt about it." She nestled comfortably against him. "I love your voice."

"Even my off-key notes."

"Even your off-key notes."

They didn't talk for a while after that. The emotions between them whirled about, the skies slowly turned grey, the stars grew brighter.

Summer 2015

John watched her walk away. His face red from embarrassment. The neighbors had been watching through the blinds. He half ran, half jogged towards her, gripping her wrist tightly.

"What am I supposed to do when the best part of me was always you?

And what am I supposed to say when I'm all choked up and you're OK?

I'm falling to pieces,

I'm falling to pieces

They say bad things happen for a reason

But no wise words gonna stop the bleeding

'Cause she's moved on while I'm still grieving"

He belted out Breakeven to the best of his ability. John never enjoyed singing, never. It made him a nervous wreck. But he still tried it, after all these years, just for her. Metilda turned around, torturously slowly, a pert smile on her lips.

"They say bad things happen for a reason

But no wise words gonna stop the bleeding."

She hugged him, tightly. It was the closest he had gotten to her in the past ninety days. John welcomed the warmth. Everything was worth it. Just for a second, to have her in his arms. He was willing to be a singer for the rest of his life.

"Why did you bring me here?" Metilda whispered, holding John's hand as he led her through the deserted house. The slightest sound made the house seem alive. She half-expected his aunt to appear from the kitchen, a tray of gingersnaps in her arms.

"Just wait."

"Is this the part where you tell me that you've been haunted by her ghost?"

He laughed, shaking his head slightly. "I just might."

"This house gives me the chills without her." Metilda shivered slightly. They walked through the dark, John's cellphone being the only source of light. Since John hadn't been keeping up with the bills, the municipal corp. had cut the supply for electricity and water.

She realized that John was taking her to the backyard. It was overlooked by John's old bedroom, where they had spent their first night together. The memory itself made her blush furiously.

The evening sun provided them some light in the backyard. John didn't drop her hand, he held it tightly as he yanked open the jammed patio door. Metilda walked out with him, the overgrown yard almost resembled a junk yard. She wondered why John had brought her here.

She watched his eyes- they were fixed with res-olute determination. "John," She eased his shoulders which were stiff with tension. "Why are we here?"

"To let go." He gripped her hand tightly, in an almost vice-like grip.

"I've been seeing her at night. Whenever I closed my eyes, she would be there, telling me to forgive you. She said she won't rest in peace until I did." John and Metilda sat at the patio steps, their hands entwined together. They had buried an old photo-graph of his aunt by the maple tree. "I hope we can bury our past resentments with this. I know it won't be easy-"

"It never was. Loving you." She was close to him. It was almost like a dream, if he gripped her too tightly she would vanish, slip from his fingertips. He had been so close to losing her. Life wouldn't have been good without her, without Louis.

"If I could go back into time, I would change everything." His voice was pained. He could still see the past pain in her eyes.

"I wouldn't."

"Why?"

She carefully angled her eyes to his face, a soft smile playing on her lips. "We fell in love again, John. How lucky are we? Not many couples are. They just drift away until there's nothing left, no emotion, just a dull ache in the chest reminding them of what once existed."

Tears welled in John's eyes. He couldn't look at her. There was a light in her, even when she had battled the darkest battle life could offer, she still clung desperately to the shore.

"I feel the same rush of our first date, except it's so much more intense. Then I didn't really know the value of what we had. Now, I've learned to appreciate every little thing you do for me. I couldn't have been more thankful."

Her eyes shone with a sudden brightness, her cheeks were flush, and her hands were warm. John knew that she wasn't lying.

Would it be a sin if he kissed her right now?

No, it wouldn't because she was his wife. John smiled and he leaned in, very slowly, giving her the opportunity to push him away. She didn't. She wound her arms around him and their breaths collided.

The first summer rain hit them as a surprise. In the gentle shower, hands found company, hearts found compassion, breaths found forgiveness, and eyes found happiness.

It was the happiest summer of John's life. His thirty-sixth summer, where he finally earned a small piece of his wife's trust.